BJORN'S GIFT

Sandy Brehl

CRISPIN BOOKS

Crispin Books is an imprint of Crickhollow Books, based in Milwaukee, Wisconsin. Together, Crispin and Crickhollow publish a variety of fiction and nonfiction for discerning readers.

Our titles are available from your favorite bookstore online or around the corner. For a complete catalog of all our titles or to place special orders (for classroom use, etc.):

www.CrispinBooks.com

www.CrickhollowBooks.com

Bjorn's Gift

ISBN-13: 978-1-883953-84-3
Juvenile Fiction / Historical / World War II / Norway
Family & Friends / Action & Adventure / Middle Grade

First Crispin Books Edition
Cover illustration by Kathleen Spale (www.KathleenSpale.com)

To readers of Odin's Promise
who insisted on a sequel.
Thank you for caring about Mari and her family
and for believing I could tell their stories.

For more about the writing and topics of
Odin's Promise
and
Bjorn's Gift,
visit:
www.SandyBrehl.com

For a glossary of Norwegian & German words
that appear in the story,
see pages 263–267.

Contents

Chapter One

Fishing the Fjord

August, 1941
Ytre Arna, Norway

Mari felt the sudden tug of another fish, a large one, and grinned. She worked the line carefully. Per leaned forward, ready with the net, causing the small skiff to bob even more on the choppy waters of the fjord.

"Take it slow, Mari. Don't let such a big one get away."

Mari's focus was on the taut line. It could be the best catch of the afternoon. Not since she was nine had she lost a fish after she set the hook. She was too focused on the challenge of landing this one to concern herself with Per's bossy attitude, but she would need his help to haul it over the side of the boat.

When it came to fishing the deep, cold waters of Sørfjord, she knew its ins and outs. She had fished, often in weather rougher than today's, for longer than she could remember. Certainly longer than her friend and schoolmate

Per, despite his constant bragging. Today, he had even wagered that he would catch more fish, but he'd lose that bet. It wasn't even close.

Mari had her brother Bjorn to thank for that. He taught her everything he knew, starting with how to read the waves and the weather. Long before she was old enough for school, he said her quiet nature made her an ideal fishing buddy. He shared his secret spots and tips about which bait to use in which season and for which fish. Now, she worked her line, letting the big one tire itself. The salty taste of the wind on her lips reminded her of those happier times before the German occupation.

She'd never best Bjorn; she wouldn't expect to. And now he was gone, hiding in the mountains with the resistance troops. Still, she was better at fishing than Per in any weather.

The huge mackerel lost its battle inch by inch.

"Ready?" she asked.

Just as it broke the surface, Per piked it, slipped the net under it, and hauled it into the boat. He whooped, "This one's huge! At least three kilos, maybe more. Good job, Mari!"

He fastened it securely to a nearly full stringer and slid it back into the water. "I'll have to prove I can out-fish you some other day. We've got plenty for now. Time to head back."

Mari nodded, grinning at his excuse. It would take a while to row to shore, divide the catch between their families, and sort out who would get an extra fish or two. This trip they could spare some small ones for a few neighbors.

They set the wooden oars in the oarlocks. The boat had a small engine, but motors were useless without gas, which had all but disappeared since Hitler's invasion of Norway a little more than a year ago.

They quickly fell into a rhythm, their oars slapping a steady cadence to quiet conversation. They were far from shore but they kept their talk to murmurs, well aware that sound travels across the water's surface in unexpected ways.

Mari leaned forward to speak over Per's shoulder. "I hope Astrid was able to work all three snare lines on her own. We need to do as much trapping and fishing as possible before school starts next week. With only four hours of classes each day, they'll load up the homework. Soon it will be too dark after school to be outdoors."

Per replied through gritted teeth. "They should just give us homework and skip the classes. Who knows what they'll try to teach, anyway."

He pulled at the oars with a vengeance, then began again. "You'll be fishing on your own more, Mari. You can handle the boat without me if you stay close to shore. I don't know what your secret is, but fish fight to bite your hook. I'll be spending my time on more important projects this fall."

Mari knew he wasn't talking about school. She was sure his spare time would be spent on local resistance activities. Her own father and brother Bjorn had rarely been home during the past year, working full time at jobs, then devoting hours and hours to . . . exactly what, she couldn't say. Codes, secret messages, graffiti, smuggling?

Per's father did the same. Mari had no doubt that Per was one of the boys who helped the cause, defying the Nazi curfew when necessary. They defaced propaganda posters, tearing them down when possible and whitewashing over them when it wasn't. She couldn't guess what other disruptions he might be involved with, all to interfere with German operations in their small town of Ytre Arna. What was once a quaint settlement on Sørfjord had been overrun by soldiers since the invasion. Ytre Arna's scenic harbors were deep and only a few hours by boat to the open sea.

Per and the others in the underground movement knew they couldn't defeat the enemy on their own. But they were determined at least to challenge the Nazi invader's smug claims of a shared Viking heritage and brotherhood.

Per interrupted her thoughts. "Any news from Bjorn?"

Mari's brother had mentored Per in resistance activities before joining the mountain fighters last June. Only her family knew where Bjorn had gone. Bjorn had told Per and everyone else that he was quitting his bank job in the village to go to University in Oslo. It was a credible story, and people often asked Mari how his classes were going. She chose her words carefully whenever she spoke about her brother.

"No," she replied to Per, her head bent to her rowing. "But even if he sent a letter, he couldn't say much that matters, could he? I know Bjorn's where he wants to be, but I wish we had a safe way to communicate. I'd feel so much better if I could write to him for advice, tell him all that's happening here. I miss him so much."

Per nodded.

Mari knew that writing to her brother could never happen with Germans in control. They read everyone's mail, listened to phone calls, followed people in the streets, and even locked up some when threats weren't enough, always looking for information about anyone who might be involved in the resistance. Bjorn couldn't be contacted, and he would never try to contact them. It wasn't safe.

Per called to her over his shoulder. "The wind is picking up, and the tide has shifted. Lean into the oars, Mari."

The two friends pulled hard in silence, and the skiff skimmed across Sørfjord, gradually approaching the homes that climbed from the shore up the steep mountainside on which they were built.

With the penetrating sun of a clear August day behind the two rowers, someone watching from shore would have seen only their silhouettes, two heads and four arms moving in unison.

As the boat closed the distance to the pier, Mari took a quick look over her shoulder. No one was visible on the roads. The two friends rowed on, accompanied by the murmur of the waves slapping against the sides of the boat.

The cry of gulls and the swoop of swallows made their setting as picturesque as a travel poster. But it was wartime. Nothing was the same as it had been little more than a year ago.

As they plowed toward the dock, Mari mulled over her mixed feelings about returning to school. She enjoyed studying. She liked the structure of school days and the academic challenges, the problems that needed to be solved. It was hard to guess, though, what Upper School would be like this year. New teachers would instruct them, not at all like having trustworthy Mr. Jensen for six years. There were rumors that Nazi sympathizers had replaced some Upper School teachers.

Most of all she worried about attending classes with students several years older, some in Year Ten. Her Lower School scores had been so high she had been promoted to advanced math, science, and literature studies. Even though her new classmates would be from local families, she felt shy about getting to know a new group of older students.

"Ease up a minute," Per said, letting his oars rock in their locks. He rubbed at his left palm, then lowered his hand into the cold water. "I've broken open that old blister." He pulled out his hand and winced as he rubbed salt water into his palm.

Mari asked, "What blister?"

He turned toward her and held out his hand, rubbing steadily at a palm that looked perfectly normal. "Don't look toward shore," he whispered. "Leif is on the pier, and he's been watching us. I think he's waiting for you."

Chapter Two

Unwelcome Neighbors

Mari couldn't imagine how Leif had found the small dock, tucked into a rocky inlet. He was certainly not there to see her. She fought her impulse to look, instead aiming her worried expression at Per's palm.

She whispered back, "What's he doing here? He lives on the other side of the mountain, beyond the school."

Per focused on his non-existent blister and continued in a low voice. "He's been strutting around the village all summer. He always lorded it over the rest of us because he's a year older. And lately he's been running with the Unghird group. He doesn't wear their brownshirt or armband—yet. He's not old enough to make it official until he turns fourteen this fall."

Mari was stunned at the thought that Leif would join *Unghird,* the Nazi youth corps. They were nothing more than a gang of thugs, strengthened by the support of German troops and local authorities. Even the Gestapo treated them as junior enforcers.

Everyone in their class understood why Leif was older than they were. He spent preschool years with his own age group, but couldn't join them when Year One started. He was kept home with some kind of illness. When he was healthy enough to return to school the following year, he joined the younger class with Mari, Per, and Astrid. But he had always preferred to associate with the boys who were closer to his age.

Per had always resented Leif, probably because the older boy's age and size difference gave him an advantage in sports and other school clubs. Even so, Per must be wrong, Mari thought. Leif would never support the Nazi Unghird.

Per dipped his hand in the fjord, shook the water off, and gripped the oars. "When his birthday comes in November, he'll wear the Unghird armband and try to ruin all of our lives, you can bet on it. Just watch what you say around him, and follow my lead."

Mari spoke her fears aloud for the first time. "The Unghird are the main reason I'm worried about going to Upper School. I never imagined one of our own classmates would join."

Per muttered over his shoulder, "You'd better get used to the idea. I just wish I knew what he's doing here."

As the skiff neared the pier, she stole glances over her shoulder to see if Leif was still there. He was. Why would he come to visit? He never gave her reason to believe he would do such a thing, although he sometimes teased. All boys did that, especially her brother.

The memory of Bjorn's impish grin tugged at her heart.

When they were close enough she heard Leif call out. "How's the fishing?" He was on the dock's edge, reaching out toward Per to catch the tie-rope. "Maybe I could join you sometime."

Per tossed it to him, hoisted himself out of the skiff, and snatched it back to lash it in place. "This little boat wobbles enough without adding more to the load. Besides, I thought you were too busy with your new friends. What are you doing so far from home?"

Mari noted the edge in Per's voice, but he was doing a remarkable job of toning down his irritation. Controlling his words didn't come naturally to him. He must have learned more from Bjorn's coaching than he had from years of Mr. Jensen's reminders.

Mari busied herself securing the oars, piling their gear on the dock, and gathering the heavy stringers of fish. If she kept her head down, she might not have to say anything.

Per nudged Leif backward and reached down for the catch. When he lifted the stringers out of the water Leif whistled. "What a haul! There's enough here for a week of good eating. How about sharing a few with me? Nothing tastes better than fresh fish."

Mari was furious. If Leif ran with the Unghird it meant his family had joined the Nazi-supporting party, the NS. If so, they were already receiving extra ration cards, better pay, and lots of other benefits. How could he dare ask for even one of their fish!

Mari's anger got the better of her and she glared up into his face. "Nei, there aren't enough for you. Three families will share these, and any extras go to the elders in town who can't trap or fish for themselves. Some are already weak from poor diets. These fish can help keep them alive. You're fit. Catch your own fish, Leif."

Per knelt on the pier, kept his head down, and shuffled their gear, making as much noise as possible and hiding his grin.

Mari imagined Leif was furious at her outburst. Instead she saw him stifling laughter, covering it with coughs. That only aggravated her more. There was nothing funny about this.

Per finally stood and turned to face Leif. "What *are* you doing on this side of the village today? I don't remember ever seeing you around here."

Mari added, "How did you even know where we'd land? This dock can't be seen from the road."

Leif grinned and reached to give Mari a hand up from the boat. She pretended to lose her balance and grabbed at a piling, then hoisted herself up on her own. Leif shook his head with a half smile, but his grin returned as he explained. "Your grandma told me where I'd find you. I stopped at your house to say hello. I'm helping Uncle Frederick move his things into his new house. But Aunt

Helene is taking forever to make some decorating choices, so I ducked out. I thought I'd say hello, and maybe take a fish home for their dinner. No hard feelings, though."

Mari's face must have revealed her confusion. Leif continued. "I thought you knew. My aunt and uncle are moving into the Jew's house across the road from yours. No one's lived in old Meier's house since he was arrested last year." He seemed happy about it all. "You'll finally have some *good* Norwegian neighbors. Uncle says he'll be needing my help to get the place repaired, so we'll be seeing a lot more of each other now."

When Mari scowled, Leif shrugged his shoulders, "See you soon," he called as he turned to leave, scrambling up the hillside path as nimbly as a goat.

Mari's shock at this news was profound. She had witnessed poor Mr. Meier being dragged down the mountain last year by a pair of soldiers, the old man's face and knees bleeding. It was her first realization of many hard truths. The German claims of friendship were worse than exaggeration; they were outright lies. It was a harsh lesson that German soldiers were dangerous enemies.

Events of the past year had revealed more shocking realities, but she never learned what had happened to Mr. Meier after his arrest. She often gazed at his deserted home and worried about him.

Mari finally sucked enough air in her lungs to speak. "Leif's relatives as neighbors? I can't believe this is true!"

From the look on Per's face, he couldn't either.

Chapter Three

Per's Request

Mari and Per sorted the catch, dividing portions for Astrid and her mother, Per's family of six, and Mari's household. For a moment Mari was tempted to claim an extra fish or two, even a small one. After all, she had hauled in most of the day's catch, and she was constantly worrying about her grandma's weight loss.

The thought passed quickly, though, since the three friends had long ago agreed to share the fish hooked on the fjord and the small woodland animals trapped in the snares according to need. When it came to berries and other "found" foods, though, the families kept their own bounty.

The climb up the path was challenging, hauling so many kilos of fish, but Per shouldered more than his share. He had always been one of the tallest boys in class, and now he was wiry thin. His limited food intake must be going entirely to bone and muscle. Mari couldn't help but admire his strength.

Despite his growth, he wasn't more than half a head taller than Mari. Her sprouting height this past year had made her one of the tallest girls in class by June. The youngest in her group, she wasn't used to that, and her skinny legs and arms felt awkward and clumsy. Still, her rowing was strong. At home, she was used to hauling plenty of wet laundry up from the cellar. She had no real trouble carrying her load of fish.

When they crested the path and it met the road, Per turned toward town.

"Wait," Mari said. "What about Astrid's trapping? She said she'd leave both our shares from the snares at my house." Per nodded and turned uphill, falling into step with her as she continued. "After we leave these with Mama, I'll help you take the fish to Astrid's and deliver the extras to—"

Before she could finish Per grabbed her arm and tugged her to his side. "Look," he whispered, nodding slightly toward Mr. Meier's cottage.

Mari scanned the sloping gravel path down to the vacant buildings and overgrown gardens that had stood deserted for almost a year. Parked there she saw an open bed truck, rusted and chipped. Clever mechanics had converted a few vehicles in town to wood-burning power, but the smelly, clunky conversion box was always evident at a glance. This truck was obviously still powered by gasoline. The Germans provided access to gasoline or diesel only for their official business or to a few select locals. NS members. Only those who joined the New Norway Nazi party and supported the puppet government could count on such favors from the Nazis.

Per's accusations were confirmed: Leif's family had joined NS, the Norway-Nazi party, and were likely high-placed from the looks of it. Mari wondered what favors and secrets they provided in exchange for an entire house, land on the coast, and a truck with the precious fuel to power it.

Then her eye caught what Per had noticed. High atop the flagpole in the center of Mr. Meier's rose bed flew the "New Norway" flag. Below that, the Nazi flag, swastika and all, flapped in the breeze.

"Let's get out of here," Mari said, sprinting ahead of Per and through the gate into her yard. She burst through the kitchen door while he waited outside.

"Mama? Mama!" Her calls went unanswered.

Per set his fish on the stone walk. He pulled a small tarp from behind a bench and covered the catch before sticking his head inside the door. "Let's take care of this first, and figure out what to do about your new neighbors later."

Mari rejoined him in the yard and lifted the latch on the sloping cellar doors. She hurried down into the laundry and cold storage space below the house. After her family's portion of fish was placed in a big water barrel, she collected Per's rabbits from the icebox.

He waited for her at the top step, silhouetted in bright sunlight. When she joined him, Per uncovered the remaining fish, folded the tarp, and stowed it behind the bench. He hoisted the fish and asked, "Are you still coming to help with deliveries?"

"I'll leave a note for Mama and catch up with you."

It was a while before Mari latched the garden gate to follow Per. Her friend was nearing the bottom of the hill where the road intersected with Ytre Arna's main street. Mari glanced quickly at Mr. Meier's house and then ran to join him, skidding to a stop on the gravel and nearly knocking them both to the ground. Per sidestepped and laughed aloud at her slide and flailing arms. "Summer is ending, but it's not skating season yet! What kept you so long?"

"When I first came out the door, I heard Leif in the yard talking to his uncle. I waited until they went back inside."

"Mari, you can't hide in the house for the rest of your life. You may as well get used to him being there and figure out how to handle it."

Per shifted his load and pulled two fish from the line. He handed one of them to Mari. They each made a delivery, and repeated the process again before they reached Astrid Tomasson's apartment. Their friend Astrid wasn't home; she was probably out walking her puppy, Thor. But her mother, Mrs. Tomasson, thanked them and took the fish eagerly.

Mari turned for home.

Per gestured for her to follow him instead. When she gave a puzzled look, he put his finger quickly up to his lips. "No questions here," he muttered, "Just come."

During the short silent walk to Per's house, Mari wondered what he wanted. But she followed without further questions.

In his home, Per stored his family's portion of the fish and rabbits, then said, "No one's home this time of day, but I want to be sure. Sit down, Mari. I'll be right back." He raced upstairs where she heard him opening and closing doors.

Whatever he was up to must involve the utmost secrecy. She wondered if it had to do with resistance activities. In a moment her friend came bounding down the steps with an odd black book clutched in one hand.

Chapter Four

Bjorn's Request

There was a lot Mari liked about Per, but his self-confidence and swagger were annoying. He played the expert in all things, even when he was obviously wrong. Now he perched on the arm of a chair, shuffling his feet and shifting the slim book back and forth in his hands. His head drooped so she couldn't see his face, and his body sagged, as limp as pickled herring.

She sat down across from him.

Waiting was easy for her. But after several minutes passed in silence she decided to speak.

Just as her mouth opened, he began. "What you said in the boat about Bjorn . . . I feel the same way. Working with your brother taught me so much. Now—well, I feel like I'm letting him down."

Mari had no idea what Per was talking about, but the thought was familiar. Both she and Per had looked up to Bjorn. Now that he was gone, off in the mountains with the resistance fighters, Mari felt she wasn't doing enough for Norway. She should be taking a stand against the Germans who seemed to be everywhere in and around her village.

The words Bjorn had spoken to her on the day he left came back to her, as they often did. "You're more ready than you know."

Ready for what? She wanted to do something important to fight the Germans. But catching rabbits and fish only amounted to surviving, not fighting.

Mari knew Per admired Bjorn greatly. For a few short months, before Bjorn had gone away into the mountains, he and Per had spent many hours together. Bjorn had served as an older brother to Per, too.

Per handed Mari the slim black book. "The day before he left for University, Bjorn gave me this. He wanted to know what he was missing here in Ytre Arna. He asked me to keep a record about what happened while he was gone."

Mari was shocked. That sounded far too dangerous.

Per noticed her startled expression and held up his hand. "He warned me to keep it hidden, not to write full names, but to try to record important events. He talked about ways to substitute words and expressions that would only be clear to us Norwegians, a sort of simple code of everyday life. He said if our house was ever searched, they wouldn't pay any attention to this little book, since it looks like a bank ledger."

He handed it to Mari.

It was a tall, slim ledger with the local bank's name embossed in gold on the black leather cover. Mari pressed it to her heart, wanting to feel her brother close again for just a moment.

Living in the mountains, coming out only now and then for swift strikes against German targets, was a risky business. The resistance fighters had gone off in part to draw the German anger away from those left in the villages, where resistance was mostly just a milder, if annoying, disruption for the invaders. The Germans were focused on searching relentlessly for Norwegian men, young and older, hiding in the secret valleys, sheltered under the granite cliffs of the Norwegian high country.

Mari lifted the ledger cover. To her surprise, she found herself turning page after empty page. The narrowly spaced lines and columns were the only marks in the book. Had Per used invisible ink?

Before she could ask, he explained. "I'm not a writer, Mari, I never have been. I have a good head for numbers. I could keep accounts of how many underground Jossing papers were printed and distributed. Or chart the shrinking ration allowances. Or keep track of the black market price for real flour—which is pointless since no one can afford it.

"But I know that's not what Bjorn wants to read when he comes home." Per looked stricken at his failure. "I'm just not good at describing what's going on in the villages. I'm not good at stories."

He looked down at his feet. "Mari, I'm letting him down."

Mari tried to lift his spirits. "If he asked you to, Per, he believes in you. Maybe you could do it if you tried."

Bjorn's parting words to her echoed in her mind. *You're more ready than you know. . . .*

Maybe that was true of Per, too.

Per looked up at Mari. "Don't take this the wrong way, but you've always been a bookworm and a good writer."

Mari smiled and nodded. Then, with a sudden shock, she realized what Per was asking her to do.

Per smiled back. "Really, you're the best writer in our class."

Mari shook her head, speechless. Finally she managed, "Nei, Greta's our best writer, Per."

"Well, maybe that's true. But she's always busy helping her father with the resistance newspapers."

Mari examined the book in her hands. She traced the tiny patterned red and blue lines of the ledger, creating columns waiting for something to fill them. She found herself recalling small stories that had occurred in recent days and wondered what she'd have written so far. What might still need to be written in the coming weeks and months?

"Are you sure? Bjorn left it for you."

She watched Per transform as his face relaxed, his shoulders lifted. He popped out of his chair and strode to the small stove in the corner of the room. "As long as he gets a report, he'll be happy."

He reached up and took something from a shelf behind the stove. "And I've still got this!" He lifted a small carving and showed it to her.

Mari knew before she touched it that it was Bjorn's work. Her earliest toys were chunky little blocks, trains, and circus wagons carved from firewood stubs by her big brother. His skills had grown as she did.

Nestled in her hands, Per's bear had Bjorn's characteristic realism in fur and pose. Its face was so specific you'd recognize it if you were unlucky enough to encounter the creature in the woods. Traditional folk carving often left a coarse finish, but Bjorn's pieces were finely rubbed and polished to a glow with linseed oil. She turned it over, knowing she'd see the initial *B,* along with a paw print carved in the base.

"Bjorn said it was to remind me that he's always with us." Per reached for the bear and returned it to the shelf.

Bears were Bjorn's specialty, since it was his namesake. The name *Bjorn* means *bear* in Norwegian. Mari had a carved bear, too, but no two of his small pieces were alike.

Bjorn had said the same to her on his last day at home, that his carved animals were reminders of all he had helped them learn.

Per's carving was of a young, strong bear, not attacking, but poised to protect its territory. Mari's bear was a cub, one he'd carved for her when she was just starting school. It wasn't as refined as later pieces he'd done, but he made it while he was still a teen. As a big brother, he knew Mari was nervous about being away from home. She carried it in her bag every day of her first year of school.

Bjorn gave Mama an elaborate carving of a mother bear with three cubs. Whenever Mama dusted it or touched it, the look on her face showed she was connecting with Bjorn.

On the first night after he left to join the mountain fighters, the first night in months that she had slept in her own bedroom, Mari discovered a carving of her dog Odin on her bedside stand. He was in classic Norwegian Elkhound pose, proud and powerful, standing guard on the mountainside. Guarding her while she slept.

Mari clutched the black ledger to her chest, then held it out to Per.

"He gave it to you for a reason. If he believes in you, then I do, too. Start with easy things, like the price of flour. In time you'll feel ready to brag about some clever way you find to mock the Nazis. But be careful how you write it!"

Per's scowl slowly shifted to a hint of a half-smile.

She clasped his hands, wrapping them tightly around the edges of the ledger. "Just remember what Bjorn's carving means. Be strong."

She got up, anxious to leave before Per tried to pass the book back to her. "I need to hurry home and start dinner. Wish me luck. Maybe Leif's gone by now, too."

She gave Per a last confident smile. "Perhaps I'll write some notes for Bjorn, too."

On her way home, she considered whether she should have taken the black ledger with her. She did feel full of stories she wanted to share with someone. But with every single step along the way her thoughts shifted to what she'd say if she met Leif waiting outside her house.

That day or any day.

Chapter Five

Mountainside Meeting

Mari's basket of raspberries sat on the grassy mountain slope, and she stretched out on her back, soaking up the August sunshine. Her hand pressed against the warm granite block marking Odin's grave. Nearly every day since her dog was killed last winter, she had made her way up the mountain to share her thoughts and feelings with him, just as she had done all those nights when he slept in her arms. The sun-baked stone was no substitute for running her fingers through Odin's dense black fur, but it helped her feel connected to him.

Her only companions were diving gulls reflected in the lake and a doe with a fawn near the treeline. She rolled onto her side and traced the letters on Odin's small marker.

"The Germans are still here, Odin. They aren't going away. Sometimes I lose hope that we'll ever get Norway back." Mari pressed the heels of her hands into her eyes, squeezing back the threat of tears.

When she opened them, her breath caught in her throat. A long shadow stretched across her legs, cast by someone standing behind her. Struggling to remain calm, she sat up and looked over her shoulder.

"You!" she cried, twisting around to swing at Per's legs. "Were you *trying* to stop my heart?"

Per danced back out of reach. Despite her annoyance at her friend's endless teasing, Mari couldn't suppress a smile. She shaded her eyes with one arm and reached out with the other for a hand up.

He took a step closer and leaned in to give her a boost. "You were supposed to meet me at the snare line. Astrid and Thor must have started without us."

Per tossed Mari a canvas tote and swung a second sack across his shoulder. "Hurry, I've got more to do today than bag rabbits and chase school girls across the mountain."

Mari was in no mood for his attitude, even when delivered with a smile. Per, Mari, and Astrid had been classmates and close friends since entering Year One together. For some reason, Per's "take charge" approach had skyrocketed recently, and was becoming even more annoying than the years of teasing she'd endured. She often just tried to ignore him, but she'd had enough.

"A few months training with Bjorn didn't make you my brother, or my boss!"

Per laughed and chattered away until they stepped into the shadows of the forest. Then his voice suddenly dropped to a whisper. "Any news?"

"Nothing good." Mari lowered her own voice to match his and scanned the shady surroundings. "BBC radio said that the Nazis are marching toward Moscow and Stalingrad. Papa insisted that the Russians would stop them in their tracks, but there's no sign of that happening."

The hopeful expression on Per's face disappeared.

Mari's throat tightened as she voiced the words she hadn't dared to speak aloud until now. "No country has been able to stop the Germans. The only reason England is still free is that it's an island. If Germany could drive their tanks across the Channel, Hitler would be sipping tea on the king's throne. How can anyone ever stop them? They conquer country after country, then drain those countries' resources to rebuild their armies. If England falls . . ."

Per gave her braid a tug. "Don't start thinking that way, no matter how bad things get. Norway *will* be free again someday."

"When? What day?" His opinion wasn't enough to convince her.

She swung her basket at the end of her arm and walked ahead of Per in long strides. It had been more than a year since the Germans invaded. Soon after her sister Lise married Erik last spring, the restrictions and laws had only gotten worse.

Mari continued to fume. "I can't even write a letter to Lise without German censors opening it and reading it. I don't know if she and Erik are safe in Oslo, or what's—"

Per slid his hand over her mouth, interrupting her

rant. Mari spun around to face him, brushing his arm away. He pulled her close and leaned toward her ear, "Shhh . . . someone's coming."

A rustling noise in the underbrush came closer. Mari saw her own concern reflected on Per's usually confident face. Had she spoken too freely where others might overhear?

A series of snorts and yips caused them both to break into grins. Thor bounded toward them, the young spitz pouncing enthusiastically from one leaf pile to the next, tossing debris and twigs aside and snatching bits and pieces in snarling little snaps.

"For such a young dog he's fierce, isn't he?" Per chuckled and knelt down, whistling two short trills. Thor raced to Per, sat, lifted his head to make eye contact, and quivered in anticipation.

Per murmured, "Good boy, smart boy. What a good dog you are." He kneaded Thor's neck and rubbed his ears while the puppy squirmed and wagged his rump wildly.

Mari joined in the petting, enjoying the feel of Thor's fuzzy cream-colored undercoat. She was more certain than ever that it was the right choice to refuse Per's gift last year and insist that her friend Astrid take the puppy instead. Astrid needed the company of the pup, and Per and Mari had pitched in to help train him. Mari enjoyed having a dog like Thor in her life, but she was determined to have only Odin in her heart.

"He'd be more impressive if he wasn't holding leaves

in his mouth like a pacifier." Mari knelt, braced herself for the weight of the young spitz, and patted her chest. "Here, Thor!" He leapt into her arms, nuzzling her neck. She savored the musky, salty smell of his skin and kissed the top of his head.

"How are we going to train him when you and Astrid keep treating him like a baby?" The mild annoyance in Per's voice was betrayed by his grin. He scratched behind Thor's ears.

Astrid joined in the petting. Mari stood up with Thor in her arms and groaned slightly. "At only six months old, he *is* still a baby, Per. But he gets heavier by the day." She gave the pup a last squeeze and set him down again.

Astrid's face beamed as she watched Thor romp and roam. When she whistled, he raced to her feet. She sank her fingers into the fur of Thor's sides. "He's growing so fast, but I worry he's too thin under all this fluffy fur. His ribs shouldn't be as easy to feel as they are. And his puppy belly is gone already. Let's get to the traps to see how many meals we'll be taking home."

The pup snuffled at the base of a tree, his hackles raised. Per laughed, then patted Mari's shoulder. "He comes close to Odin in brains and spirit. As a spitz, he shares some of the same Norsk Elkhound ancestors."

Mari focused on Thor and managed a smile. "I worry, though. His protective instincts could get him in trouble the way they did with Odin." She pushed back images of the day her dog had been shot by a German soldier. "Thor needs to be perfectly trained . . . or the same thing could happen to him."

An uncomfortable silence hung in the air until Per finally spoke to Astrid. "I thought Mari made us so late that you'd have checked *your* snares and *ours* by now."

"I've learned a lot from you and Mari since you started teaching me to trap this summer. But I worry when I work the lines on my own. The rabbits should be dead when we check, but one day I might find one struggling or crying. I don't know what I'd do. If I don't set the snares correctly that could happen, couldn't it?"

Mrs. Tomasson earned few ration cards in her clerking job, and Astrid needed to help feed Thor, so trapping was a survival skill she was anxious to master.

Mari admired how far her friend had come from the quiet girl she once was. She marveled even more at changes in herself. Just a year ago she had known nothing of the village resistance movement, and she had trembled in fear at the slightest threat or worry.

Now it seemed she had aged a decade, and she seldom felt the stomach queasiness that once plagued her. Nevertheless she struggled to understand who in the village could or couldn't be trusted. The more she learned, the more guarded she became. It felt safer to trust only family and the closest of friends.

They hiked a network of trails on the face of the mountain while Thor bounded around their feet. When they reached the start of Mari's snareline, Per took charge.

"I'll work Astrid's line with her before mine. I want her to realize how good she is at collecting and resetting the snares. Mari, if you finish first, come find us."

Then he added, "Or should I check your snares, too, Mari? If you aren't having much luck, maybe you could use some coaching."

Astrid and Mari reacted at the same time, scowling and shoving Per's shoulders. He stumbled backward, taking a few wild steps and waving his arms like a windmill. Then he steadied himself and laughed. "Sorry. I was just trying to be helpful. Suit yourselves. It's your dinner tables, not mine."

Astrid and Mari looked at each other and rolled their eyes. Per was full of himself, as always. But his help with the snares was invaluable.

As Per, Astrid, and Thor disappeared into the woods, Mari turned to her own path into the mountain forest. "Go on, you two. Keep your eyes open for berries and nuts. The wild brambles are nearly picked bare already. I'll catch up when I finish my line."

Chapter Six

School Worries

Later the trio reunited and settled by a small stream for a break before heading down the mountain. Per scooped a handful of water from the rushing brook and swallowed hard, forcing down the last of his coarse bread. "Not a bad day," he said, making a move toward Mari's basket. But she anticipated his familiar ploy and snatched it away.

"Gather your own berries, or nibble Astrid's. She's got a talent for spotting every stray berry on the mountain!"

Astrid quickly shifted her own basket out of his reach.

Thor was napping nearby. He woke to look at the threesome, sniffed, yawned, and then settled back to sleep with a sigh.

Astrid massaged the back of the young spitz's neck. "When school starts Monday afternoon, we'll need to check our snares in the mornings."

Mari nodded, gnawing steadily on the last bite of

what passed for a sandwich these days: coarse bread with a smear of fatty lard. The quality of the Ytre Arna villagers' food—poor grain for bread, little or no butter—was pitiful.

Unless, of course, you worked with the Germans, like Leif and his family.

"Why are you two always so lighthearted when it comes to school?" Per dug the toe of one shoe into the stones near the stream. "We have to settle for Year Seven classes in our old building, while German soldiers make themselves at home in *our* rightful places in the Upper School buildings."

Neither girl answered. Mari noticed Astrid biting her lower lip and massaging Thor more vigorously.

Per used the heel of his shoe to shove dirt and stones into a larger and larger mound. His jaw was clenched as tightly as his fists.

Mari shook her head. "I don't like their rules either, but maybe it's not so bad. Since the Germans claimed our Upper School buildings to house more troops, we won't be in classes with students from Indre Arna and Garnes. I know a few of them, but not most. It will be easier to know who to trust this way, don't you think?" She was offering them arguments she had made to herself since hearing about the changes.

The "New Norway" government was directed by the Germans in the shadows who were really in charge of everything the government did or said. In mid-summer, they announced a nationwide change in school schedules. Students would attend in shifts. Lower School for younger children would start earlier, and end at noon. Upper School would start at 1:00 and end at 5:00. The short schedules freed up room in the school buildings for other use by the occupiers.

Per's foot smashed the dirt piled near his feet. "Nazis living right in our schools! Can it get any worse?" Startled, Thor sprang up, circling Per's legs and barking.

Astrid wrapped her arms around Thor's neck, trying to calm him. "Mr. Jensen says this is just the beginning. We have to make the best of it." She held Thor close, told him to sit, then pulled his collar and leash from her pocket. He squirmed while she fastened it.

They gathered their things to start for home.

Mari spoke up, following Per and Astrid. "She's right, Per. Even though we'll have new teachers, we can go to Mr. Jensen for the truth."

Per led the way toward the path, keeping his voice low. "We see him all the time in Ytre Arna. We don't need school for that."

Mari said nothing. Her two friends lived in town. And Per was practically the town crier. They both knew more of what was happening.

Since school had ended in June, Mari had seldom encountered other classmates or Mr. Jensen. Her home was at the edge of town, and she spent her free time fishing or on mountain walks to check the snare lines and visit with

Odin. She walked into the village almost every day, but as early as possible. There were few German soldiers in town during morning hours, and she avoided idle conversation with locals. After sharing coded updates with loyal neighbors, news heard the night before on her family's hidden radio, she weeded her portion of the community garden in the village square or waited in ration lines for their family's meager allotments. Then she hurried straight home.

Norway's new reality was dismal enough without spending time in town. Street signs and business displays had been changed to German. Propaganda posters were plastered everywhere. Most people walked about grimly with their heads down. It was as if the energy and cheer of her familiar village had been crushed by countless military boots and wiped away by those horrid swastika flags.

Even when Mari joined Astrid and Per on their mountain outings, they could seldom speak freely. Food rationing left everyone but Nazi sympathizers scrambling to survive, so people of all ages roamed the hillsides at all times, gleaning berries, mushrooms, and greens like mountain goats. Too often a German squad of soldiers would pass within sight, sometimes intent on patrols, other times appearing to be out for a leisurely stroll.

Like everyone else in town, the threesome limited their conversations, especially complaints or news updates, to whispers in isolated moments, or when safely behind closed doors.

Sudden shouts and scrambling pulled Mari from her thoughts. Thor had bolted after a squirrel and pulled the leash from Astrid's wrist. Per whistled two sharp trills and Thor skidded to a stop. The pup hesitated, swiveling his head from Per to the escaping squirrel. Thor retraced his path, dragging the leash behind him. He plopped down at Per's feet, eager for approval.

Per held his open hand before Thor's face, then turned to check on Astrid. She had tumbled forward onto the path before the leash slipped off her wrist and was brushing small stones from her knees and shins.

"Are you hurt?" Mari asked. She reached for Astrid's hands, checking the palms for scratches or cuts.

"I'm fine," she laughed, "but Thor must be gaining more weight than I thought!" At the sound of her laugh Thor jumped up and down, yipping.

"Sit!" Per commanded in a stern but quiet voice, repeating his hand signal. Thor immediately dropped to a sit, his face showing the same pleading look he had a few moments before.

"He didn't mean to hurt me, Per. Don't start bullying him. We get enough of that from the Germans." Astrid knelt at Thor's side and stroked his forehead and back, resulting in wild wagging and panting.

Per's voice was nearly as stern as it had been with Thor when he spoke. "His life could depend on obeying commands, you know that." He shot Mari an apologetic half-smile before he continued.

"He'll be smaller than Odin once he's grown, but his nature will be the same. He's bred to guard a herd rather than hunt, but he's a protector at heart. If he bolts or growls or seems at all threatening to a soldier, it could be the end of him. He needs to learn to obey while he's young."

Mari stepped between the two of them and folded Thor in her arms, blinking back the salty wetness stinging her eyes. "You're both right. In a few more months Mr. Molstad will adjust Odin's old harness to fit Thor, and make a stronger leash, too. Don't worry, Astrid, no one's going to see him as a threat while he's still such an adorable puppy."

Thor wiggled himself loose from her hug, shaking vigorously before lying down at Astrid's feet. That seemed to settle the matter. Astrid picked up his leash, they gathered their things, and headed down the path.

Chapter Seven

Fireside Reflections

Mari shivered. An evening storm chilled the blistering August day. She unwrapped her wet hair and toweled it thoroughly. The comforting fire in Bestemor's stone cottage reminded her of better times. Mari bent at the waist and shook her head over the hearth.

Her grandma's voice tugged her back to the present. "Come, little one, I'm tired tonight. I'll go to bed as soon as we finish."

Mari smiled, no longer offended by her childhood nickname. It was used from habit and affection, not to treat her like a baby or exclude her from important secrets. Not since last year.

Her grandma set a comb, hairbrush, and scissors on the arm of a chair, then eased herself into it. Mari settled at Bestemor's feet, rested her chin on her knees, and gazed into the flames. Grandma's fingers untangled her freshly washed hair and felt normal, safe. Mari's shoulders slumped and she leaned back against Bestemor's legs with a deep sigh.

Not much in the past year felt normal. Or safe.

Her eyelids drooped and she inhaled the tang of wood smoke. It triggered memories of life before the German soldiers occupied Norway. Mari's thoughts roamed through images of those days, more than a year ago, as if paging through a family photo album: dinners with an abundance of food and laughter; the handsome face of her grown-up brother Bjorn; Mama's smile, her blue eyes sparkling under a forehead uncreased by worry; Papa's hair still dark like her own, with only dustings of gray on his mustache.

Her mind's eye sought out Odin, and in her memory he was there near the kitchen door, his sleek black coat nearly hiding him in shadow. His eyes were closed, but his nose twitched ever so slightly, alert for any tidbits tossed his way. Bestemor bustled from stove to table, refilling bowls with meat and vegetables, wiping drips of buttery sauce with the corner of an apron tied around her ample waist.

All were happy and healthy.

A tangle in her hair tugged Mari back to the present, to the reality that the village of Ytre Arna had been forced to deal with since the German forces invaded, claiming to be friends.

Her thoughts turned to Bjorn: tall, strong and always smiling. Since he left more than two months earlier, she worried about her brother constantly. Mari's imaginings about Bjorn's activities were more frightening than reassuring.

Occupation took a toll on everyone. In just one year of rationing and fear, her grandma's comforting curves had melted away so much that Mari felt Bestemor's sharp shinbones press against her back.

Mari slid her hand behind her and rubbed her grandma's leg, brushing against the scar on the older woman's calf. "Bestemor, you're losing too much weight. I'll bring you some currant jam when you finish."

Bestemor chuckled and stopped combing long enough to rub Mari's earlobes. "None of us eat well these days. At least I had plenty of padding to lose. I haven't been this slim since I married your grandfather. That jam would ruin my girlish figure!"

She nudged Mari's shoulders. "Besides, we'll need it later this winter. Now lean forward, Mari, so I can trim the ends."

Bestemor combed Mari's waist-length brown hair against the towel across her back and clipped the ends. "We'll toss these in the yard tomorrow for the squirrels," she said, dropping bits of hair onto a small cloth. "At least *they'll* be able to keep their nests warm in the winter."

Mari had come to depend on the good humor Bestemor managed to display even in dire circumstances. Her grandmother often found something to joke about in the barrage of news and propaganda spread everywhere by

German-controlled sources.

Mari was less able to find the humor in their situation. The sight of posters and official Nazi reports glorifying the success of Hitler's forces infuriated her. She was disgusted by their declarations that Norwegians had "welcomed" the German occupiers as "Viking brothers," superior to all other races.

"Anything important on BBC tonight?" Mari asked.

Her family and a few others in the village risked keeping illegal radios to listen to daily reports from Britain. Mari had missed the broadcast while finishing chores, and Bestemor hadn't mentioned anything.

"Nothing that we hadn't heard earlier," Bestemor said. "After the last few days, let's hope no news is good news."

Many in Ytre Arna relied on a few families, like hers, who had dared to hide their radios. They found ways to secretly share honest news, confirming or contradicting the Nazi claims of grand and endless success.

The title of the Nazi newspaper, *Fritt Folk,* mocked the fact that Norwegians were no longer "Free People." Only fools believed that. But their village had such fools, a number of weak-minded Norwegians who were helping the Germans in return for favors. Families like Leif's were always snooping around, listening to conversations, eager to run to the Germans to report on the activities of anyone who was loyal to Norway.

Defying the radio ban was a risky choice. Since she learned of her grandma's hidden radio a year earlier, Mari had shared those risks, delivering coded messages on her morning walks into town, but only to those who could be trusted. Even though she was only twelve years old, she would suffer the consequences alongside the adults if their efforts were uncovered.

Mari half turned toward Bestemor, whose opinion she trusted above all others. "Since Hitler's sending his army into Russia, he'll need to pull soldiers out of Norway to help fight Stalin, don't you think?"

Her grandma exhaled slowly and eased her granddaughter's shoulders forward. She twisted Mari's hair into an elaborate braid, her fingers working as skillfully as they did when she crocheted or embroidered. She finished quickly, gathered the equipment into the damp towel, and set the bundle in her lap. Mari waited, longing for reassurance.

She jumped at the sudden snap of a burning log dropping through the grate. She swung around and covered her grandma's hands, desperate for a response. "Bestemor? Things *will* get better soon, won't they?"

Her grandma hesitated, eyes closed. For several minutes the only sound in the room was the crackling of the fire.

"I wish I could tell you that, baby girl, but you deserve the truth. Germany seems determined to take over the world, one country at a time."

Mari leaned closer, afraid of what Bestemor might add.

"It shocked the world when Hitler broke his agreement with Stalin and invaded Russia in June. Who knows what he'll do next? His forces must be stronger than anyone knew. Tens of thousands of soldiers invaded us last year, taking over Norway in just a few days. Since then their numbers here have more than doubled. None of us imagined any of this was possible. But here we are, living with the unimaginable."

Mari squeezed Bestemor's hands, desperate for a more optimistic report.

Her grandma smiled. "There's always hope. We know King Haakon is busy in England planning a counterattack with the Allies to rescue Norway. Hitler seems to believe that, too. He doesn't want to lose his 'Northern Fortress.' That's why he has sent more troops and equipment here."

Mari leaned into her grandma's outstretched arms and clung to her. Bestemor whispered into her ear, "Whatever happens, Mari, you'll survive. We all will. As long as we don't lose hope. Now, we both need to get some rest."

With Mama and Papa at a meeting in town until late, Mari welcomed an invitation to sleep that night on Bestemor's couch in the cottage.

Chapter Eight

Unghird Pressures

Autumn, 1941

Once school resumed, Mari travelled into town each day. The soldiers had established routines, and she no longer felt a rush of panic when she saw them on their patrols.

She worried more about encountering Leif or anyone with an Unghird armband than she did about Hitler's troops. Those teenage Norwegian boys, barely older than she was, were determined to impress the Germans. Even though they had no official authority, Unghird members relied on numbers and surprise to make trouble. Complaints from those who suffered their taunts, bruises, or property damage fell on deaf ears. The Gestapo had warned the local police not to intervene.

To make things worse, a few of the older, brown-shirted, armband-wearing boys were in each of her classes. Under the watchful eye of teachers, they behaved normally. During the short breaks, though, they were drawn to each other like magnets to an iron cross, obviously up to no good.

Mari often saw them corner younger boys, questioning their courage, pressuring them to join Unghird as soon as they turned fourteen. They praised the *Führer* and the traitor Quisling, the Norwegian leader who helped Germany rule Norway. Refusal to consider joining the Unghird led to threats. Mari wondered how long it would be until the brown shirts resorted to physical attacks right on school property.

Just that morning she noticed Leif, who was still not an official member, at the fringe of one group in the hall of the school building, cajoling, bullying, and boasting as much as the rest of them. She heard him brag that he was counting the days to his birthday in November when he could wear his own uniform and armband for the first time. Mari changed direction to avoid the boys, hoping he hadn't seen her.

But when she turned the corner she noticed him step away to follow her.

She ducked her head and hurried down the hall.

"Mari, wait!"

She kept her head down and continued another few steps before she felt him grab her arm.

"What's the hurry? We don't return to classes for fifteen minutes."

She looked up at Leif, inches away, and realized he was even taller than Per. It was no wonder he was so welcomed by the Germans. His hair was as yellow as a baby chick, and his eyes as blue and deep as the fjord on a cloudless day. He could have been a model for a Nazi propaganda poster.

"Mari, what in the world is wrong with you? I asked how your classes are going, but you act like you didn't hear a word I said."

She rubbed her temple and squeezed her eyes shut.

"Are you ill?"

All she wanted was to get away, but this was making matters worse. "I'm fine," she said, shrugging her arm free from his grip. "My studies are really intense, and I get headaches. I just need to get a little air before chemistry begins."

"Oh, I'm sorry to hear that. You're used to being first in the class, but you'll catch up in no time." He glanced back at the Unghird group moving down the corridor. "I've got to go, but I'll see you soon."

With that he turned and sprinted to rejoin the pack.

The positive side of Leif's devotion to that group was that it kept him too busy to visit his aunt and uncle often. To her great relief, once school was underway, Mari rarely saw him at the house across the road from her home.

At the end of each day Astrid and Mari stuck together, often joined by another friend, Greta. The three girls hurried on their walks home, at least as far as their routes allowed. On Thursdays, Unghird held official meetings with a German officer after school, so the girls could look forward to stealing a few moments once a week to talk.

Once they were out of sight of the school, they stepped off the path and ducked into the shadows of the trees.

Astrid scanned the area thoroughly, then leaned forward and spoke softly. "I didn't realize Unghird had so many members. And such bullies! Is it this bad in other districts?"

Greta, as always, knew more than the others about town politics. Greta's father was involved in writing the underground newspaper, the Jossing papers. So this was a great chance for Mari and Astrid to get a good dose of reliable local news.

Greta shook her head. Her voice was quiet but reassuring. "The cities are worse, but inland rural districts are not as bad. I don't think we should worry too much. Papa says it's the new members who are the worst, trying to impress the older ones with their toughness. Most of our boys won't join, you'll see."

Mari asked, "But when eligible boys refuse to join, won't they be attacked?"

Astrid nodded, a hint of panic in her voice. "She's right! Per and the others in our class will turn fourteen by the end of the school year."

But Greta's calm expression gave the other two a glimmer of hope.

"Most will refuse. But a few may have to sign up. Even if they don't want to." She signaled them to step a bit deeper into the shadows and lowered her voice further. "Knut's father is postmaster. Mr. Bruland pretends to cooperate with the Germans, and even joined NS. He has the trust of many officers, so he can share information with the resistance. He can secretly pass or inspect special pieces of mail from time to time. So . . . it would seem suspicious if his son doesn't join Unghird on his birthday."

Mari's breath caught in her throat at the thought of it. Mr. Bruland's friendliness to the Germans had angered her last year until Bestemor reassured her that he supported the resistance. Now, Mari's daily delivery of coded radio news often included him. The idea that his deception meant Knut would have to join the Unghird group was hard to accept.

Trying to figure out who could be trusted made Mari's head spin. At least those like Leif's family, who flew the New Norway flag openly, were known to be traitors. The only safe approach was to trust no one unless she was certain they were part of the resistance.

Greta signaled to wait and took a few steps to the path, looking toward school. She hurried back. "Shhh . . ." Her warning was barely audible, but her hand signals were unmistakable. The index finger covering her lips shifted as her open hand cupped behind her ear. All three girls strained to listen, then hurried back to the path to head for home.

Mari forced herself to keep her eyes straight ahead, despite the sounds of rowdy voices and crunching gravel not far behind.

Astrid and Greta launched a conversation about homework in voices that sounded surprisingly natural. Mari's mouth and throat felt as chalky as what passed for flour those days. The Unghird meeting must have ended early. It was all she could do not to sprint down the slope to town. She might be able to reach Mrs. Nilsson's where she could stop for a visit before they caught up. She knew, though, that running would trigger a chase as surely as Odin would respond to a darting rabbit.

She was jolted back to their situation by Astrid's elbow in her ribs. "Right, Mari?" Astrid's expression conveyed her apology for the jab but pleaded for Mari to respond. "Your homework is even harder than ours and takes forever to finish, right?"

Mari did her best to use a natural voice, despite her dry mouth. "Ja, hours every night. Even though the year just started." She ran her tongue across her teeth and swallowed hard. "My teachers said they understand it's harder for me because I've skipped ahead, but they won't take that as an excuse for less than the best." With the sound of voices and gravel nearing them, she realized what this conversation was about.

The girls hitched their bags higher on their shoulders and called good-byes at the turn in the road.

Greta added cheerily, "Hurry home, then, to get started." She waved and jogged toward her father's pharmacy, where she'd likely spend hours helping him prepare the next issue of the Jossing papers before starting on her own homework assignments.

Astrid's route matched Mari's for a short distance further. She began jogging, too, and called back at Mari, "Your legs may be longer, but I'm faster!" She bolted ahead, but Mari answered with her feet and caught up quickly, soon matching Astrid stride for stride. Her brown braid and Astrid's golden one bounced on their backs as they built speed and neared Astrid's corner. They slowed slightly as they approached, and Mari conceded in a louder voice than necessary, "You're fast, that's for sure. But I'll train harder and beat you next time."

Running, even downhill, soon left Mari with a stitch in her side and her breath coming in gasps. At a bend in the street Mari slowed to a jog and dared to look back. With no uniforms in sight, she dropped to a rapid walk to avoid attracting attention from soldiers who often appeared in town at dusk.

By the time she neared Mrs. Nilsson's house she was breathing normally and had seen no Unghird uniforms. Bestemor's lifelong friend was sitting near the window, as always, and offered a wave and a smile. The steep homeward climb from there was short and familiar, and Mari hurried up the last stretch to her house.

She was almost home when she heard an unpleasantly familiar voice behind her.

Leif's.

"Wait, Mari."

Chapter Nine

Questions Without Answers

Mari slowed, but continued toward her gate, now within sight. She called over her shoulder, "I'm late, Leif, I can't talk tonight." She hoped he was on his way to his uncle's house and only wanted to say hello, as she had managed to avoid running into him all day at school.

He ran in a burst and caught up with her. "You'll want to hear the news from tonight's meeting. I'm on my way to Uncle Frederick's house to tell them, too."

She was desperate to turn and run, but wanted to know what had him so excited. With her feet shuffling toward the gate, she asked, "What meeting? You aren't old enough to join Unghird."

He beamed a wide smile at her and puffed his chest like a strutting rooster. "I will be, soon. Edvar is a unit captain. And we've been friends since preschool. He lets me come to the meetings now, so I can become a squad leader soon after joining."

Mari turned aside and coughed, hiding her irritation. Leif's buoyant attitude reminded her of the classmate she once thought she knew. But his words distorted that memory. She pictured him leading a pack of bullies as they goose-stepped through the streets, singing Nazi songs. Worse still were images of friends and neighbors being taunted and harassed by the gangs he might organize.

She took another few steps, dropped her backpack into one hand, and reached for the gate. "If it's that important, please be quick. I'll never finish my homework if I don't start soon." She swung open the gate and stepped into her yard, pulling it shut before he could follow. She swung her pack into her arms and clutched it to her chest, putting a barricade between her and whatever his news might be.

He closed the distance between them, bouncing slightly on the balls of his heavy shoes. "I'll give you the short version for now. By tomorrow the posters will be all over town, and at school, too, with all the details. The meeting ended early so the members could help put them up, but only those in uniform can participate. Edvar said I should tell as many people as possible."

Mari dreaded what he would say, but her family needed to know. "What is it, then?"

He spilled it out so fast she struggled to keep everything straight. What he said triggered memories of the panic she felt when she saw Mr. Meier being arrested. She pushed those memories aside to make mental notes of every word Leif uttered.

"It's finally official tomorrow, September 19. The NS will enforce new laws to control the Jews."

Leif rattled off details like a wish-list fulfilled. "Jews must have a 'J' added to their passports so they can't leave the country. In fact, they have to get written permission from the Gestapo to even leave their own villages."

Mari was stunned, not just at the ridiculous new regulations, but at the puzzle of why the Germans cared about Jews.

Leif told of other new rules to forbid Jews from living with or marrying non-Jews, or even owning businesses. There were more, Leif told her, but she was relieved when he stopped, waved goodbye, and hurried across the road to Mr. Meier's place.

It would *always* be Mr. Meier's place, no matter who lived there.

She thought of Sarah, who had been in her class until a year ago. No matter how much she missed her best friend, Mari was more grateful than ever that Sarah's Jewish family had moved north in the early days of the occupation. She said a silent prayer that they had continued on and crossed over the border to safety in neutral Sweden. She wished every Jew in Norway had done the same.

Last year when Mari asked how many Jews lived in Norway, Bestemor said there were very few, especially outside of Oslo. There were only a few synagogues in the capitol, and the small groups of Jews living in other parts of Norway gathered in homes for prayers on holy days. Why were the powerful Germans so threatened by a few hundred Jews spread across their vast countryside?

Mari hadn't given a thought to who was or wasn't Jewish until the Nazis arrived. Now, posters constantly blamed Jews for anything and everything bad, no matter how ridiculous.

But why was Leif so jubilant about the new rules, as if it were some enormous victory? The laws were unfair, even hateful. If Hitler and the Nazis hated Jews so much, why not just let them leave the country if they wanted to go?

None of it made sense to Mari.

News updates around the table usually waited until after the meal ended, but that night Papa started the discussion while their soup was still hot. Mari expected Leif's report to be the most important news shared, but somehow Bestemor and her parents had already heard about the restrictions. Before Mari could ask any questions, a more serious issue was discussed.

Papa folded his arms on the table and leaned in. "Hitler has launched a massive increase in occupation forces. The Gestapo captured an Allied message with plans to invade Norway, supported by King Haakon's army based in England."

Bestemor chuckled. "It's about time! We've been waiting for some real help since last year." The words seemed bitter, but her tone was lighthearted. "If the Allies let us know when to expect them, I'll trade my jewelry for flour and coffee and invite them to a party."

Mama sounded more worried. "Have you heard where an assault might happen? Where will German reinforcements be sent? To the northern coasts? To Oslo?"

Papa shook his head. "We must expect more soldiers everywhere, including Ytre Arna. The Nazi attacks on Russia have been so successful that Hitler can send more troops to Norway to protect the ports all around our coast. My sources think more than a hundred thousand Germans are already here. But they are saying that will double within the year."

The numbers were staggering to Mari. She tried to picture doubling each and every soldier roaming her village and district.

Then a sinking thought came to Mari. Where would the extra soldiers stay?

Mama confirmed her worst fears. "Hitler has been planning this for a while. The searches, inspections, and even our Christmas 'guests' last year weren't just scouting for radios and contraband. They were identifying places to house more soldiers."

Papa had already been notified of what was coming. Mari's home was on the list. With three bedrooms upstairs in the main house, Mari was going to have to sleep downstairs with her parents—so troops could use the entire upper floor for living quarters.

Instead of climbing into bed that night, Mari paced her room. Her fingers clutched Odin's driftwood stick. His gnawed tooth grooves had been worn smooth from recent months of bedtime rubbing. She stared at Bjorn's carving of Odin, perched on a shelf nearby.

Picking up the carving, she felt suddenly connected to Bjorn, across the miles, somewhere out there in the mountains. He was seldom wrong about anything. But right now Mari was sure he was mistaken to say she was ready to handle whatever might happen here without him for advice and protection.

Her pacing and fretting continued until a little after midnight, when Mama brought her a cup of mint tea, then sat on the bed by Mari's side to gently rub her back.

"Get some sleep, little one. Morning will come too soon. And tomorrow is a school day."

Mari rarely missed school, but what did it matter? "There must be something we can do, Mama! How can we live in this house with soldiers? With Nazis? With weapons?" She gripped the bedcovers in her fists and fought back tears. "And why isn't Bjorn here to help?"

Mama eased herself to the edge of the bed. Putting first one foot then the other on the floor, she rose as if in slow motion. Taking the cup from Mari, she examined her daughter's face. After a long silence, she spoke.

"Mari, I understand how you feel. Helpless. You are not."

The determination in Mama's voice was unfamiliar.

Typically soft-spoken and gentle in tone, this was different. "We are powerless to change our circumstances. But we always have the power to choose our path.

"Each can do something. Bjorn. And Bestemor. And your father and I. We choose courage. And loyalty. And strength."

Mari's head drooped and she felt ashamed of her fear, but felt it nevertheless. It was not an easy thing to ignore.

Mama reached out and tilted Mari's chin up to look into her eyes. "Your family is here to love and protect you in every way we possibly can, but how you face these changes is *your* choice.

"Bjorn believed you were strong enough to choose well, and so does Bestemor. Papa and I do, too."

Mari closed her eyes, trying to shut out everything that lay ahead for them. She heard Mama turn out the small light and walk to the door. "Try to get some sleep. Nothing will change by morning, and you can face the day better if you rest."

The door clicked shut. Mari sat in the dark for hours before drifting into a troubled sleep just before dawn.

Chapter Ten

Surrounded by Soldiers

October, 1941

The thought of living in the same house with German soldiers overwhelmed Mari. Then, she had an idea. Mama and Papa discussed it with Bestemor, who readily agreed. Mari's relief was enormous.

She would live with Bestemor in the cottage after the soldiers arrived.

Within a few days, though, Papa took her solution a step further. Soon after, preparations were underway.

It was no surprise that the local German commander applauded her father's proposal. Papa offered to empty out and make available *all* the rooms of the main house, upstairs and down, storing the family's furniture and belongings in the garage.

Papa and Mama would move in with Bestemor, too.

The cottage's little dining room was turned into bedroom space for Mama and Papa. Small packing cases were stacked along the walls to hold their clothing, bedding, and other necessities. Papa hung a rod across the arched doorway to the kitchen, and Mama sewed a heavy blanket to provide the semblance of a door.

Mari would share Bestemor's tiny bedroom. Bestemor's bed was taken out and two smaller beds were squeezed in. Bestemor's largest pieces of furniture were stored in the garage. Of course, the linen chest, with its forbidden radio hidden in the base, remained in place on the back wall.

Initially Mari had asked if she might make a bedroom of her own in the cottage attic. Her parents exchanged grins, and Bestemor chuckled, leading the way to the pantry. Mari rolled the flour barrel away from the corner and moved the broom to lean it against a shelf.

Her grandmother waved toward the rungs attached to the wall in the corner. "I haven't climbed this in years, but you remember how to open the hatch, don't you? Maybe you'll find some happy memories hiding among the dusty old boxes."

When she was too young for school, Mari had loved scrambling up to play there on bad-weather days, boosted up with help from her babysitter, Bestemor. Now, the minute she propped up the access door and peered up into the attic, she realized why they were laughing.

She swung herself up from the top rung into the dusty space and sat on the smooth wooden floor, careful not to bump her head on the sloping roof. Even seated, the center ridgepole nearly touched the top of her head. From there the raw timbers angled down to meet the walls. As a little girl, she ran around freely, but she'd grown so tall her only options were sitting, kneeling, or crouching.

Mari peeked over the edge of the hatch at her family, grinning up at her from the pantry. She joined their laughter when Bestemor wagged her finger at Mari. "So now you're willing to share a room with an old woman?"

Mari descended, brushing cobwebs from her hair, then hugging her grandmother. "No wonder the soldiers aren't demanding that space for themselves. When did you lower the roof?"

Hot mint tea and more laughter settled the matter. They'd all be living within inches of each other with very little privacy. But at least they wouldn't be sharing the main house with German soldiers.

Mari wiped her sweaty forehead on her flannel sleeve. For late October it was surprisingly warm. Hauling boxes and furniture had her considering a change to summer clothes, but they were packed away somewhere in one of the boxes. She leaned against a disassembled bed frame and viewed their progress in the garage.

Papa had sold the car the week before, along with any equipment that required gasoline or diesel fuel. Once their furniture was stacked and crammed into that space, the garage seemed to have shrunk.

Removing most of the family's furniture from the main house allowed the soldiers to fill rooms with simple cots, makeshift desks, and a long barracks-style table for serving meals. The house could then hold as many as a dozen Germans. At least with this arrangement, Mari wouldn't have to picture soldiers sleeping in their family's beds or eating at their table.

Mama and Bestemor would cook and clean for them. In return, the commander promised extra ration cards and leftovers. Whether or not they'd keep those promises was anyone's guess.

Voices outside the garage caught Mari's attention and she hurried to help. She saw Mama and her grandma struggling with a heavy box. Mari slid into Bestemor's place and took over her share of the load. "Mama and I will get this. There's room for it near the window."

Mari grunted slightly and shifted her left hand to get a better hold. "Bestemor, can you get the door for us? Be careful of the loose gravel."

They maneuvered into the crowded garage, shuffling between narrow stacks to reach a massive sideboard, an old piece of furniture that had been in Papa's family for generations. A blanket protected its mahogany surface.

"Wait, Mari. We'll need Papa's help," Mama said.

"We can do it," Mari said. "I'll lift my side first, Mama. Being tall is a good thing sometimes. One . . . two . . . three!"

With Bestemor helping Mama hold the other side,

Mari grunted and heaved one corner of the carton up onto the buffet. She slid her hands to the other end, boosting it in place. Bold lettering on the box caught her eye: *ALBUMS AND PHOTOS*.

"This feels more like the good china and silverware." Images of Jul celebrations with their finest dishes arrayed for a traditional smorgasbord filled her mind.

Mama nodded, running her hand across the label. "If someone decides to steal something, they might skip a box holding only family memories."

Bestemor led them out of the garage. On the path back to the main house she looped an arm around Mari's waist. "Give me a boost to keep my weary bones moving."

Mari returned her reassuring hug. It would be an adventure, all of them living together. She hesitated to ask the question that was foremost in her mind.

How long would they live this way?

She didn't ask, because the answer was obvious.

No one knew.

Chapter Eleven

Sunday Surprises

Mari woke early Sunday morning, aching from head to toe. Arctic winds erased the previous day's heat overnight. Mari shivered, added a wool sweater to her flannel shirt, and tiptoed into the kitchen to the rhythm of Bestemor's snores. At the stove Mama stirred something that smelled rather good. She looked over her shoulder at Mari, nodding toward the small table.

Mari lifted the sturdy mug waiting there and sipped.

"Oh, chicory! What's the occasion?" She inhaled deeply, cradling the mug with both hands. Coffee had long since disappeared. The tiny ration they received was bartered for more essential foods, replaced by mint or other teas made from local plants. A year ago, she would have turned up her nose at steeped chicory, but now it was a luxury. Its savory richness offered a pleasant reminder of real coffee.

Mari reached for a bowl from the shelf and sat

down. A large dollop of a bubbling, porridgey something plopped into Mari's bowl. It was impossible to identify, but it smelled tasty. Her mother's nose crinkled with a half smile. "Don't ask me what to call it until you try it. I wish we had cream or sugar, but at least this will fill you up."

Mari blew on a spoonful and took a tentative taste. *Not bad.* She held the mass in her mouth for a moment and then swallowed. She summoned a weak nod. "It's nothing like *rømmegrøt* or oatmeal, but it's better than dry toast. What is it?"

Mama served herself a small bowl before returning the pan to the stove. "It's what's left of yesterday's stone-loaf."

White flour was scarce, rationed in small portions for families with children under two. That left most of the villagers to deal with a brownish, chalky powder, used in place of whole-grain flour. It produced tasteless, brick-like loaves with gummy centers. They refused to call it bread.

Mama continued. "The stone-loaf was too dry and hard to chew or slice, so I soaked it last night. I planned to use it in a meatloaf for dinner, but the cold morning inspired me."

Mari took another taste and detected a bit of honey and some berry flavors.

Mama examined a spoonful of the concoction, wrinkled her nose again, and tasted it. "What it is, I guess, is *filling*. It's something for your stomach. These days that's as much as we can hope for."

Mari polished off the rest of her chewy porridge, took

her bowl to the sink, and kissed the top of Mama's head. "It was a treat. Only you could make stone-loaf cereal out of cement."

Bestemor joined them. She must have overheard their discussion. "I wonder if cooking it this way will cause fewer fireworks than it does as bread!"

They shared a chuckle. There was little hope that even Mama's cooking could offer relief from the gassy side-effects caused by the chalky additives in flour substitutes.

Mari pulled on her jacket. "Is Papa up and working? I'm ready to help."

"Ja," Mama said. "He went down to the garage before first light. Send him up for breakfast." She served a small portion of the cereal mix to Bestemor, who rubbed her stomach and offered an exaggerated expression of pleasure.

Before the door clicked shut behind her Mari heard her grandma make an equally exaggerated farting noise, followed by the comforting sound of their laughter.

In the dim garage Mari looked around for her father. Stacks blocked most light from the windows, and lines of sight were nonexistent as she made her way through the narrow aisles. She called out, "Good morning, Papa. Mama has breakfast ready at the cottage."

When there was no answer, she returned to the doorway to look for him. Had he climbed down to the pier to welcome the sunrise? He was nowhere to be seen, up or down the path. She stepped back into the garage.

"Papa?"

"Here, Mari. I heard you before but didn't answer." Papa was standing at the end of an aisle in the far corner of the garage.

Mari was sure he hadn't been there a moment ago.

"Come, Mari, I have something to show you."

When she reached him, he touched her lips in a "shush" gesture. His brow was furrowed, as if something serious was coming.

Mari's lighthearted mood from the kitchen disappeared. She felt the gloppy porridge settle in her gut like a bullfrog, gurgling slightly.

Papa led her deeper into the corner and stopped in front of a weighty-looking stack of boxes solidly wedged between adjoining walls of furniture. He released her hand and signaled again for silence. He looked toward the door, then knelt beside the stack of boxes, grasping the bottom one. Shuffling first one way, then the other, the stack slid out from the wall, inch by inch.

Mari couldn't believe her eyes. She was often impressed by Papa's strength, but after packing and moving boxes for weeks, she knew how heavy even one case would be.

When he had the stack halfway into the aisle he gestured for her to kneel beside him. He must need help to move them further.

She braced herself and gave as firm a tug as she could. The stack slid out easily, wobbling slightly. She fell backward and would have banged her head on the bedposts behind her if Papa hadn't steadied her.

They were almost weightless! What could be in them?

"Papa—"

He signaled again for silence, then motioned her out of the way. He pulled the stack farther from its carefully constructed wall space to block the aisle. He reached toward the garage wall, gripped a bent nail, and tugged.

Nothing happened, of course. Why would he try to pull out a nail without a hammer or claw?

He gripped again and tugged, twisting slightly. This time the boards forming the bottom half of the wall swung toward them, revealing a dark, shallow space.

"It's time you learned the truth, little one."

He crawled inside and she followed. For several minutes, the beam of Papa's flashlight led them through a narrow aisle.

She struggled to listen as Papa pointed to various contraband and forbidden items, but her mind was busy trying to envision where she was. On one side was the original wall, built up against the side of the mountain. On the other side of the hidden aisle was a false wall. Outside of that, her family's furniture and boxes were stacked to the rafters, disguising this hidden space. No wonder the garage had filled up so quickly.

Both walls of the secret space were lined with small shelves holding wrapped bundles, a variety of hunting guns, and boxes of ammunition.

"Let's go, Mari. Mama's waiting for us."

She shook herself free of the thoughts tumbling through her head and followed Papa through the half-wall opening into the dim morning light of the garage.

Papa gestured for her to back up while he closed the hatch, then he slid the stack of boxes back into place.

He stood and took her hand. "We need to go back to the cottage. It's important for you to know about this. After breakfast I'll show you more. Don't say a word about this to anyone, understand?"

She nodded. "Ja, Papa."

For once she was too overwhelmed to have questions.

Chapter Twelve

Preparing for the Worst

They stepped out onto the path. After the dim light of the garage, the bright morning was disorienting. Mari was startled by an unexpected but familiar voice.

"There you are, Mari. I was looking for you everywhere!"

It was Leif.

He bounded toward them and stopped abruptly, blocking their way to the house.

"Uncle Frederick just told me the news!" Leif's grin made it clear he was thrilled about something.

Papa rescued her. "What's giving you jackrabbit legs, Leif? Mari and I are late to breakfast, and Mama's patience has its limits. Mari, run ahead and tell her I'll be right along. Leif and I will sort out whatever it is that has him so excited."

Mari flashed a grateful smile at Papa and bolted like a fawn.

Her thoughts about the secret space were forced aside as she hurried to the cottage. Instead, worries about Leif tumbled and troubled her. The classmate she once knew was nearly unrecognizable to her now. He had changed so much. She managed to avoid him at school most days, but he seemed intent on finding her whenever he visited his aunt and uncle.

She couldn't risk making an enemy of someone who could threaten her family. When he appeared she let him do all the talking. When he said upsetting things, she clamped her jaws tight and bit her tongue. And in all his chatter, he sometimes would reveal useful information about what the Germans were up to.

If only he were more like Per, a loyal Norwegian boy, she might have welcomed Leif's company.

Bestemor scooted her chair even closer to Mari's and wrapped her arm around her granddaughter's shoulder, pulling her close. The cottage was never meant to accommodate all the people and furnishings that it now contained. When her family sat together in the tiny kitchen, elbows bumped.

Papa continued sharing Leif's news.

"A full squad of soldiers has been assigned to our house. Along with a pair of officers," he paused to sip his tea. "They are specially trained to find transmitting radios, English spies, and other resistance operations."

Mari's voice faltered, barely getting the words out.

"Wh-what about Bestemor's radio?"

Papa reassured her. "Ours is a *receiving* radio, Mari. It picks up any broadcast within range, including those from England. It's illegal because it doesn't lock out everything except the Nazi broadcast station like the radios NS members receive.

"The special unit will hunt for radios that send messages to the Allies about things like troop movements. The German equipment is designed to locate *transceiver* radios, ones that can receive *and* transmit signals. The soldiers will never know we're getting BBC reports behind their backs."

Mari searched her grandma's face and breathed more easily at the sight of her confident smile.

Papa's next words erased that fleeting comfort.

"Of course we must be vigilant. Remember when a Gestapo collaborator infiltrated a resistance spy ring in Televåg last April? The Germans dynamited or burned most of the village to the ground. Those who weren't shot are now in prison."

Mari felt the pain in Papa's voice. Rumors had circulated that a neighbor had collaborated with the Nazis, betraying members of the Norwegian *Linge* spy group. Mari couldn't believe lifelong neighbors would do that to each other. Within days, though, official Nazi papers carried photographs and printed names. Papa knew several of the victims. The Jossing papers reported the same details.

"There've been other rumors since then, which Leif just confirmed. The increased German forces in Norway are eager to track down all spy cells. Allied advance scouts are sneaking into the country, so Germans are monitoring all access points for an invasion."

Papa looked at his family, huddled together in the small cottage. "Our fjord is considered an ideal route for small boats to enter undetected. All the villages of Sørfjord will have to house more German soldiers in the coming months."

He put down his mug and rubbed at his temples before speaking again. "Leif thought we knew all this. He assumed we were making our house available because of its perfect location on the fjord. He thought maybe we had even joined NS."

"*NEI!*" Mari's response was as much a cry as a shout. She wanted to run out of the room, but she couldn't even squeeze her way out from behind the table. "What can we do, Papa? Now he'll never leave me alone."

Her family wouldn't support the Germans. How could Leif think that? How could anyone think that?

"Mari, I told him he's mistaken. I said we moved to the cottage to keep our privacy, and only that. I said what the soldiers do while they're here is not our concern, as long as we can still fish the fjord and go about our business."

Mama gripped Papa's arm. Her voice was steady but her hand wasn't. "Did he believe that? Does he suspect our involvement with the resistance?"

"He was disappointed, certainly, that we hadn't decided to join NS. But it didn't seem to dampen his high spirits. He jabbered on about getting to know the special team, learning how they work, and how he'd be joining Unghird in a few weeks."

Papa squeezed Mama's hands between his, their heads together, whispering.

Bestemor patted Mari's arm, humming softly. Mari closed her eyes and leaned on her grandma's shoulder.

When a chair scraped the floor Mari's head jerked upright. Mama refilled their cups and then stood behind Papa, gripping his shoulders. "We need to set aside this news for now and discuss how we'll live when the soldiers move in. Once they arrive we won't be able to talk as freely, even when we think we're alone."

Bestemor added, "Tomorrow I'll have extra keys to the cottage made in the village. We'll each carry one, and even when we're home, the door must be locked at all times. We can't risk having soldiers walk in during private discussions."

"Or dig through our things while we're away," Papa agreed.

Planning took more than an hour, after which they got back to work.

Mari imagined Papa's secret space in the garage as a private escape, a little retreat where she could hide and pretend for a while that the outside world was the way it used to be.

A truly safe place.

But Papa's instructions eliminated those thoughts. He spoke softly but left no room to question. "Bjorn helped me build the false wall after the invasion began. After the Germans ordered us to turn in weapons, they conducted house-to-house searches. We finished just in time to prevent them from confiscating everything we had.

"My best hunting rifles, some ammunition, and a few other weapons are hidden there. I turned in a few old items, so the Germans wouldn't get too suspicious. Other things that were outlawed are stored there, too. Many in the village have done the same thing, but we must never speak of it to anyone.

"Smaller valuables and family heirlooms, the few remaining after bartering last year, are hidden in Bestemor's attic. The time may come when they'll be traded, too, but only as a last resort. If those items are discovered, our only crime is hoarding."

He added, "If the garage space is found . . . I'll claim full responsibility to spare all of you from blame."

Mari started to protest, but one look from her father made her swallow her words.

"The garage space must be kept secret," he continued, patting Mari's hands. "It was important to show you, but you must never go there, and deny any knowledge of it, if questioned. I'll enter and leave the garage routinely, but I'll only use *that* space if necessary."

His words and knowledge of the dangerous contents kept in the secret storage area caused everyone in the room to fall silent.

Then, with a sigh and creak of her old joints, Bestemor rose to her feet and refilled the kettle, setting it on the stove to boil.

That night Mari missed having a room of her own. There she could thrash about, get up and pace, and think aloud. After years of talking to Odin, she still found that giving voice to her worries calmed her, even if no solution was found. With Bestemor within arm's reach, she struggled to lie still and work things out in her head.

Ever since the occupation began her parents insisted that the less she knew, the safer she would be from suspicion or interrogation. She realized it was essential for her to know about the garage before the soldiers moved in. She couldn't go about the yard or house searching for her father if he was doing something in that hidden space.

Still, every new secret she learned felt like another target had been pasted on her back. What if the soldiers coming to live in the main house wanted to ask her questions? What if they found her shyness and silence suspicious?

No date was set for the Germans to arrive, but Leif's chatter had suggested it would be soon. Walking through the empty main house before bedtime, picturing it as a military barracks, had nearly broken her heart. She helped Papa slide a cabinet over the access door in the pantry that led to the basement, so the only way in and out of the cold rooms below was through the cellar doors in the yard.

She'd be working down there nearly every morning, helping Mama with laundry, while a house full of Germans lived right above her head.

She rolled onto her side and took several slow deep breaths, hoping she could adjust to such a terrifying reality by the time they arrived. Reviewing the day's developments only agitated her more. She slid her hand under her pillow, searching for Odin's chew stick.

Bestemor's gnarled hand stroked Mari's forehead and cheek.

"Are you sick, baby girl? You've worked hard all weekend, and you're dealing with harsh truths." She propped up on one elbow and leaned toward Mari. "I could fix you some tea. Mint might help."

Mari squeezed her grandma's hand. "I'm just tired, that's all. It *was* a long day. I'm sorry I woke you."

Bestemor chuckled. "You must be deep in thought to believe I was sleeping. You didn't notice I wasn't snoring? Let's call a truce with the trolls of wartime for tonight and get some rest."

Mari rubbed Odin's driftwood. "Ja, sleep would be welcome."

"I love you, little one. School day tomorrow, so *sov godt*."

"You sleep well, too, Bestemor, I love you."

Mari expected to lie awake for hours, but with Bestemor's thumb stroking her hand she was asleep before her grandma's snores began.

Chapter Thirteen

Hiding in Plain Sight

At first there were ten in the house, but a week later soldier number eleven showed up. Feeding them and cleaning became Mama's full-time jobs, with Bestemor helping out. For her part, Mari worked out a routine that provided the least likelihood of dealing with them.

The Germans were obsessive about avoiding contagion and illnesses, demanding clean clothes, towels, and bedding much more often than reasonable hygiene required. While Mama and Bestemor prepared and served their breakfast, Mari straightened Bestemor's crowded cottage and then headed down into the cold-storage cellar beneath the main house to start the laundry.

When she had time, she helped haul loads of clean clothes to the cottage to fold or iron. If any time was left, she climbed the mountain to visit Odin and check the snares. When weather was favorable, she did some fishing, especially on weekends.

The services her family provided to the soldiers earned

them extra ration cards and leftovers, so the need to gather food wasn't quite as desperate as it had been before the squad of Germans arrived.

Most days, as soon as Mari's morning tasks were complete, she'd wrap a simple lunch and take her school things to the library in town to do homework. Assignments weren't as difficult as she feared, but visiting the library served another purpose. If she walked to school from town, Leif was less likely to find and join her.

When he spoke of anything other than the Germans, he was as friendly and familiar as ever. But the minute Unghird members arrived, or when he discussed topics about the occupation or Hitler, Leif became someone she barely recognized. It was impossible for Mari to relax in his company.

After the soldiers moved in, Leif spent more of his free time at Mr. Meier's house, even inviting himself into Mari's yard to speak with the soldiers living there. They often lounged in the garden, smoking their seemingly endless supplies of cigarettes. On the very day Leif turned fourteen he showed up wearing his Unghird shirt and armband. His bragging and swaggering taxed Mari's self-control to the limit. Around him, she clenched her teeth to keep angry words from escaping, making her jaws ache and her temples throb.

When Mari complained about Leif, her family offered sympathy, but caution.

"Never forget, Mari, he has powerful friends now. It's

dangerous to show your anger." Bestemor rubbed Mari's shoulders and reminded her granddaughter how easily her expressive face revealed her true feelings. "I can always tell when you're upset with *me*, little one."

Mari protested instantly. "I'm *never* unhappy with you, Bestemor. Never."

Her grandma chuckled and tugged Mari's braid. "Yes, you were, just minutes ago when I urged you to be friendly to Leif."

Mari squeezed Bestemor's hand. "But I'm not really upset. I know you're trying to keep me safe."

Bestemor squeezed back but repeated her point. "Baby girl, your face mirrors your honest emotions. I hate to ask you to hide those. For your sake, though, and all of ours, you must practice a kind of acting that disguises your anger and distrust."

"I'll try, Bestemor. I really will."

Papa worked long hours. Likewise, Mama's jobs at the house kept her busy until late in the evening, often relying on Bestemor to help as well. Mari wasn't comfortable being alone at the cottage, even with the door locked. When she could, Mari watched and counted to be sure that all eleven uniforms had marched away for some drill or mission, but long after the sound of their boots faded into the distance she felt she was being watched.

Mari had a twinge of regret at not granting Per's request to take over writing to Bjorn in the bank ledger.

Instead she began using a small notebook of her own, writing "letters" to Bjorn, but ones she would never mail. She reported on changes at school and the new laws. But in the little cottage, finding a safe time and space to write was a challenge. She tried writing a bit when she was home alone but always ended up trembling and stuffing the notebook away after only a few lines.

She wanted to protect the rest of the family so she hadn't told them about it, or the ledger. She was careful to write in a way that would seem innocent to outsiders, but she knew that Bjorn could read between the lines, understanding what was happening to the quiet town of Ytre Arna. Still, she couldn't shake the feeling that while they were all away working or at school that someone had been poking through their things.

To guard her secret, she created a lining in her backpack where she hid the notebook and carried it everywhere. Hiding it there where she could keep a close eye on its whereabouts seemed less risky than leaving it in the cottage, but still made her very nervous.

Chapter Fourteen

Censorship

November, 1941

On most mornings Mari had the library to herself. Old Mrs. Kaland stayed in her office, working or nodding off behind her desk. Amid the musty upholstered chairs and waxy tabletops, the constant grip of anxiety eased enough that Mari felt comfortable writing to Bjorn there.

One morning she shifted in her chair, scoured every inch of the room, then fumbled with her backpack. Deep in the fold of the lining her woolly red *nisse* cap grazed her fingertips. Germans were so aggravated by the symbolic caps that they openly complained and confiscated them. They claimed "red" knit caps showed support for communist Russia. Mari hadn't worn hers after that proclamation, but it was satisfying to carry it with her. She reached past it to pull out her small notebook.

Even in the solitude of the library, she wrote only a

few minutes at a time. Afterward her shoulders and neck ached with tension. She always planned ahead what to say and how to say it, finishing as quickly as possible.

Crouched over the page, clutching the pen and making notes in neat curling letters, her pulse pounded in her ears. Mari wrote for as long as she could control her nervousness, eyes darting to the door after every sentence.

Before writing that day she read over her past "letters." She was reporting rumors and news: bunker construction along the coast, success on the Russian battlefields. Her words sounded almost like bragging about Nazi progress. This might be a safe approach, but was it what Bjorn would want to know?

That morning she chose to write about a bright spot in family life, Lise's anticipated holiday visit in a few weeks. She didn't mention her hopes for contraband foods, but just said that Lise returning home would remind her of the year before. She was sure Bjorn would know what that meant.

Mari returned the notebook to her backpack and sat in silence, surrounded by the sights and smells of hundreds of aging books. She took out Lise's latest letter. She was careful not to tear it, the folds creased from repeated reading. Mari had so much to tell Lise and hoped her sister wouldn't have to cancel her plans for a Jul-time visit. Lise was clever. She might help Mari create a code system to use when writing for Bjorn, or have advice about how to deal with Leif.

BAM! BAM!

Mari was shaken from her thoughts by the sound of the double library doors banging against the walls. Light streamed in through the doorway, framing two silhouettes.

Mari's eyes were riveted on the figures as she inched backward into the shadows of the stacks of books. Two Unghird members stepped into the lobby. Mari edged forward, tugged at her backpack, and slipped Lise's letter in it. She slid her chair under the table, lifting it slightly to stay silent, straining to hear what the two young men were saying to the librarian.

"Read the list while we get started. Any books you failed to remove will be confiscated and destroyed."

Mari hurried to the children's corner where she hoped to stay out of sight but hear what was said. The two young men in their brown uniforms had come to enforce recent orders: all Norwegian history and cultural books were banned—from public places as well as homes.

It was one more step by Germany to erase Norwegian identity. Classes in German history, government and arts were added, replacing Norwegian studies. A special class on the mastermind of Nazi beliefs, Karl Marx, was mandatory. During the summer months, to the surprise of the students and teachers, school shelves had been emptied of books about Norway's language, culture, and heritage.

Just as Ytre Arna's street signs and shop signs had been replaced with ones printed in German, orders were issued to replace Norwegian language with German, beginning in the earliest grades. But teachers had refused to comply. Classes were still being taught in Norwegian, although older students studied German language.

To protect their home library, Papa had packed away most of their Norwegian literature, leaving a few harmless novels and reference books in the house. The forbidden books were wrapped in waterproof oilskin, boxed, and hidden in the garage.

The sound of heavy shoes moving through the library's nonfiction section pulled Mari back to the present situation. Books were slammed on tables, each louder than the one before. A voice demanded answers in a mix of German and Norwegian, "An order was sent to you more than a week ago! Why are these still on the shelves?"

Recognizing the village teens, the librarian complained, "You're talking gibberish. Use the language you've known since birth. I don't speak German, and I know nothing about your orders."

Like nearly every adult in Norway, Mrs. Kaland was quite capable of reading and speaking German. In fact, she was fluent in several other languages as well. A common resistance tactic was in play: claiming any failure to follow rules was because of misunderstanding or confusion.

Mrs. Kaland scolded the Unghird boys as if they were toddlers, warning them not to make so much noise and cause such a mess. A glance at the wall clock informed Mari she'd be late to school if she didn't leave soon. There was no other exit, so she needed to gather her courage along with her backpack and walk right past them. She hoped they'd finish quickly, but there was little chance of that happening from the sound of things.

Should she make her departure noisy enough not to startle them, or try to slip out while they were busy reading titles? She tightened the straps on her bag and looked up to find Leif standing in the doorway. His expression indicated he was as startled as she was.

"Mari, what are you doing here?" he asked in a garbled mix of German and Norwegian.

"Homework. I'm going now, or I'll be late to school," she stammered, stumbling forward and trying to squirm past him through the doorway.

He took only half a step back, barely enough space to let her pass. "If you wait, I'll walk with you."

She didn't speak but shook her head and tried to move on.

"Hurry then, be on your way." Leif's voice was gruff, but quiet, and she noticed that he looked toward his partner on the opposite side of the room. That's when she realized he was with Edvar, the captain of his Unghird unit.

"Ja, I'm going now." Mari lowered her head and rushed out the door, resisting the urge to run. Her long strides propelled her up the cobbled streets and she glanced over her shoulder every few steps to see if anyone was following.

Chapter Fifteen

Friends Change

The German studies classes were the only ones that Mari attended with classmates her own age. Mari took comfort in spending time with them again, although Leif's Unghird transformation tainted her memories of their earlier years together with Mr. Jensen. Was she wrong about their long past friendship? Had her innocence blinded her to his true nature during those years together? She couldn't remember him being like he was now. He *had* changed.

What could possibly have caused him to adopt such hateful Nazi values? She recalled Greta's report about the postman's son, Knut, who wasn't yet fourteen; he would be forced to join Unghird to avoid suspicion about his father's loyalty to NS. Leif had no such pressure. His family supported the Germans one hundred percent. That apple had not fallen far from his family tree.

Mari wondered if the uniform itself might hold some

power over anyone who wore it. Might it change young Knut, too?

German soldiers or officers' wives were brought in to teach German studies. Twice a week, Frau Bauer led them in traditional Germanic and Third Reich songs and poetry. She was a softspoken woman and quite talented on the piano.

Classes in the arts had always been Mari's favorites, but the subject matter of these sessions disgusted her. At least she had ample opportunity to practice Bestemor's advice, masking her true feelings and controlling her tone of voice.

That afternoon Mari concentrated on singing the lyrics to "Deutschlandlied," the German anthem, without rolling her eyes or scowling. Then Leif entered the class, late. Frau Bauer stopped playing, and Leif snapped to attention at her side.

"Excuse my late arrival, Frau Bauer. I was engaged in actions to support the Führer." Then his arm swung out and he declared, "*Heil, Hitler!*"

The teacher returned the salute with less enthusiasm and resumed playing the song's introduction while Leif made his way down the aisle. Mari stared at the wooden desktop but Leif stepped right up to her.

"You should thank me for not detaining you at the library. We need to talk," he growled. He turned on his heel and sat in the chair in front of her.

The next twenty minutes were excruciating. Mari

stumbled her way through the verses without giving a thought to the lyrics. Why exactly did he need to speak to her? What had she done wrong to warrant his attention?

When class finally ended, she joined the line and repeated in unison, "*Danke, Frau* Bauer." Leif was just ahead. As he stepped through the door, she hoped he had forgotten and moved on. With only one foot in the hall, though, Mari felt his hand grip her elbow, and he led her to a nearby bench.

She pulled her arm free and asked, "What's so important, Leif? My chemistry class is next. I can't afford to be late, not the way you can."

"You won't be late, Mari. But you'd do well to consider why I have such privileges and change your attitude. About me, and about our new way of life. I could help you . . . or hurt you."

"What are you saying?"

She took half a step backward but Leif pulled her pack from her shoulder. Was he suspicious? Would he search her bag and find the notebook? Panic seized her, and she struggled for breath.

"What, Mari, what's wrong?" His voice was intense. Was he mad at her, or worried for her?

He dropped the backpack on the bench and put both hands on her shoulders. Her knees buckled and she sat down, gulping for breath and clutching her bag.

Leif sat beside her. "Are you ill? If Per were here you'd tell him what's wrong, wouldn't you? I've been your friend as long as he has, why won't you trust me, too?"

Why not, indeed. She searched his face for the classmate she had known for years. When her eyes dropped to his armband, her face must have revealed her thoughts. He frowned.

With heavy traffic in the hall she should resist telling Leif what she was thinking, but the truth spilled out. "I'll never be able to trust you again."

His face was close enough to hers that she saw his jaw clench. His voice was barely audible. "Grow up, little girl. Things aren't always what they seem. I thought you were smart enough to figure out how to survive in our new nation." He tugged at his armband. "We never asked for this. Wearing it doesn't change who I am."

He nodded toward the uniformed soldiers at the end of the hallway. "This is our life now. *Your* life, too. Some of us choose to side with power, and reap the benefits. Others fight it, and suffer the consequences."

Mari glared at him, no longer trying to hide her feelings.

His voice stayed low, but his words pummeled her like fists. "Then there are those who lack the courage to choose. Like your family. You eat better than others, your lives are safer than many, and you make the Germans right at home in your house, cooking meals, doing their chores. Still, you feel superior, judging others. Judging me."

How could he say that? How could he even think that? Her face burned as if she'd been slapped.

"Look at you," he continued. "You're not yet thirteen, but you compete with students years older. Use that brain of yours. When I asked you to stay at the library today, it was so Edvar would tell the others you're my friend and leave you alone. I was offering to help you. When will you grow up and see that life's not all black and white, good and bad? Inside you're still a baby. Only a baby would think as you do."

When his speech ended he stood, hooked his backpack over one shoulder, and started to his next class. He stopped suddenly and called to her. "Hurry, little girl, or you'll be late to class."

Mari sat in stunned silence, sorting out her fears and anger. She was furious at his accusations. Even so, she recognized nuggets of truth in his rant. There was little in her life that was certain, except this one thing: she had made an enemy of someone who could harm her and her family.

Leif was out of sight by the time she stood, her knees trembling. She managed to slip into chemistry class just seconds before the door closed.

When she left at the end of the day she passed Leif with his Unghird gang. This time he glared at her, making no effort to mask his feelings. Her frantic walk home included frequent checks over her shoulder and a desperate grip on her backpack.

Chapter Sixteen

A Room of Her Own

Mari rushed into the yard, relieved to find it empty. A quick glance at the kitchen window of the main house revealed Mama and Bestemor serving the soldiers their evening meal. It would be two hours or more before they'd return to the cottage, and Papa rarely arrived home before her bedtime.

Mari's pulse hadn't stopped racing since her encounters with Leif at the library and then later at school. Fumbling with the key to the cottage only made things worse. Once she was safely inside with the lock clicked, her grip on the backpack eased and she breathed normally.

Leif's challenge made her realize that carrying the notebook with her was a mistake. Hiding it from Mama, Papa, and Bestemor had seemed like the best choice, but if one of them walked through the door at that moment she would pour her heart out and beg for advice.

Instead, she was on her own.

She yanked the notebook from her pack and ran into Bestemor's bedroom. Before she could cross the crowded room to the linen chest with its hidden radio, she stopped herself. The notebook was a problem of her making, not something to add to her family's secrets and burdens.

She spent the next hour opening and closing cabinet doors, pulling out drawers, and checking for loose floorboards. She explored the bathroom from floor to ceiling and even poked around the furnace room. Each corner and cranny was ruled out for one reason or another.

Mari sat at the table with a cup of tea and nibbled a chunk of stone loaf smeared with lard while she reviewed in her mind every meter of the cold cellar and laundry in the main house. There were possible hiding spots there. But knowing soldiers had free access to every part of that house convinced her the notebook would be safer in the cottage.

Her last hope was the pantry.

The pantry itself saw too much use, with Bestemor and Mama knowing where every can, carton, box, and jug was supposed to be. But the pantry offered access to another possibility.

Moving the flour barrel and broom aside, she used the attic ladder to reach the hatch on the ceiling. She lifted it and stuck her head up into the attic. When she had dismissed the attic as a suitable bedroom, she wasn't thinking of it for any other purpose. Papa had said he stored family valuables somewhere up there. And it just might offer a solution to her dilemma, too.

She climbed up and entered on her knees. Moonlight streamed through the window, revealing a bulb on a nearby support beam. Just as she was about to pull the string, she stopped herself. The windows had no blackout curtains, and a light could be seen from the road or from the garden at the back of the house. That was a chance she couldn't take. She'd only be able to use the space during the day or with the light of the moon.

Soldier's voices in the garden meant supper had ended. Mari spotted a rolled carpet runner near the hatch and unfurled it toward a nearby trunk along the wall. She crawled on the carpet to the trunk, lifting the lid just enough to slide the notebook inside and closing it quickly. Then she backed up to the hatch, careful not to disturb cobwebs or leave marks on the dusty floor beyond the highly patterned thick wool rug still spread out on the floor. If anyone bothered to check the attic, it would look as if nothing had been touched in years.

Within minutes the hatch was closed, the pantry was restored, and she was at the stove. She sipped tea while stirring soup for Mama and Bestemor's return. For the moment her panic was reduced to a simmering worry. She could keep her writing secret for another day.

In the following weeks Mari developed a new routine. Instead of going to the library after her chores were complete, she spent time in the attic. Alone in the cottage, first she'd double-check that the main door was locked, then set out a cup of tea and an open book on the kitchen table. The nearly empty flour barrel and the broom were moved aside so she could ascend and enter the attic.

After crawling onto the rug, she'd prop the hatch so it was barely open. If anyone came to the cottage door, she wanted to hear in time to reach the pantry floor. She practiced, and found she could be down, with the hatch closed behind her, in the time it would take someone to clomp onto the small wooden porch outside, unlock the door, step inside, and remove their boots for softer indoor slippers.

For a few minutes each day she wrote to Bjorn.

Never for long.

Never saying anything that could be used against her family.

Day by day she began to relax, writing for longer times, some days filling an entire page. When her anxiety built up, she'd slip the notebook into the trunk and return to the kitchen.

Eventually she was comfortable and curious enough to follow her writing with short explorations of the attic. At first she remained on the carpet and did a visual survey: the stone chimney at the center of the attic; boxes large and small, some labeled, some not; large posters or framed art wrapped in butcher paper and propped along one wall; odd pieces of furniture lined up at the far end of the attic.

One morning after cleaning the cottage she hauled the dry-mop and dust rags up the attic rungs. Her curiosity compelled her to explore more thoroughly and the only thing keeping her from it was worry about leaving a trail through years of cobwebs.

In very little time she had ducked, shuffled, and hunched her way from one end to the other, swiping the floor, beams, boxtops, and miscellaneous items. She'd half expected to unearth nests of mice or a family of hibernating bats, but the entire space was snug and secure, free of droppings or other evidence of wildlife intrusions.

She returned to the hatch and surveyed her work as dust motes floated through the diffuse light from the small windows. A musty stillness remained, creating a convincing appearance of an unused storage space. She felt comfortable and secure in Bestemor's attic, satisfied that there she could share her thoughts with Bjorn.

Chapter Seventeen

Lise Returns

December, 1941

Mari had never been so eager for a school break. She spent two full days cleaning Bestemor's cottage and helping Mama prepare special recipes that the Germans requested for their Christmas celebrations.

Somehow soldiers never lacked now-scarce ingredients that were once part of Mari's daily life: flour, sugar, butter, eggs. Mama had seen them wrapping packages of luxury foods to send as gifts to Germany. They reveled in Norway's comparative abundance, and Jossing cartoons showed scrawny soldiers now bulging out of their uniforms after only a few months in Norway.

It was no wonder that supplies for locals had all but disappeared.

While she worked, Mari worried if Lise might cancel her visit. Her sister and brother-in-law planned to travel first to his family's farm in Norway's midlands, then continue on to Ytre Arna, but circumstances could have changed. She had written that she'd come for a couple of days *if she possibly could*, but her last letter was several weeks old.

Mari was anxious to get Lise's advice about dealing with Leif.

About her notebook "letters" to Bjorn.

About so many things.

Mari kept her hopes up and decided she would wait all day at the train station if necessary.

The morning train came and went without them. The noon train did the same. Mari's resolve faded in late afternoon when the station swarmed with soldiers, many toting bundles and holiday packages. She would rather wait for the evening train at the library, but she hadn't returned there since that day Leif and Edvar appeared.

Instead she sunk onto a bench in an out-of-the-way corner.

Memories of last year's visit helped pass the hours. She didn't expect her sister's suitcase to hold rare treats as it had the previous year; rationing and restrictions tightened month by month, as more German soldiers poured into Norway. All Mari cared about was seeing Lise again.

When the last train was due, Mari found a seat on a bench closer to the platform. She eyed the wall clock, comparing it to the posted schedule. Soon sitting still was out of the question, even though her pacing drew attention from milling Germans. By the time the train squealed to a stop and its doors opened she was frantic.

If Lise and Erik weren't on this train, they wouldn't be coming at all.

A stream of uniforms exited with no sign of her sister. Mari's heart dropped to her socks. Then she glimpsed a familiar face approaching, nearly hidden behind a German soldier.

Mari reached her just as the uniformed young man turned to Lise, grinned, and set a large suitcase at her feet. Her sister smiled and exchanged a few words in German before the soldier departed.

Lise threw her arms wide. "Are you too grown to hug your big sister?"

Mari rushed into her arms, holding on a long time. Finally the two sisters separated. Lise smiled and looked at her bulky suitcase.

"I'll need your help with this. Erik stayed behind with his family." Together they hauled Lise's case to the street and loaded it on a small cart from home. Mari examined the suitcase and even sniffed.

"Yes, little one, there are a few treats inside. Let's leave them there until we're all together."

Mari's mouth watered at the thought of foods that she hadn't tasted in months, but she focused on the luxury of a few hours with Lise all to herself until Bestemor, Mama, and Papa finished their long workdays.

Lise's bag was soon settled next to their grandmother's bed. "Bestemor insisted we share her bedroom. She'll sleep on the sofa while you're here. It's only two nights, but I wish you could stay longer."

They sat on the floor near the hearth, warming up and holding hands. Lise pumped Mari for details about what had happened in Ytre Arna since her wedding in May.

It was common practice everywhere in Norway for soldiers to move into private homes, so Lise said she hadn't been too surprised to hear about that. She surveyed the crowded but organized spaces in the cottage and nodded her approval of Papa's plan.

"This little cottage makes a cozy home, and keeping the whole family away from the soldiers is brilliant! It's awful that your new neighbors are NS, but that's happening everywhere. Vacated properties are given as prizes to the few who side with the invaders. Did you ever hear what the Germans did to dear old Mr. Meier?"

"Nei," Mari said. "For a few months the Gestapo kept a small camp of prisoners near town, but then everyone was loaded up and moved. Papa says they were sent to Bergen. Some say to Oslo, or even Germany. If he knows anything more he won't tell me." Each time she pictured the two German soldiers arresting her Jewish neighbor on the mountain, her heart ached.

Lisa squeezed Mari's hands. "Papa protects all of us, not just you, Mari. He carries more secrets than we can ever imagine, but he does it for our sakes."

Mari nodded and hid a grin. It was satisfying to know the secret in the garage before her sister did. Lise had only been home for a short Christmas visit and her wedding weekend since the invasion, so Papa's project would be a surprise.

They talked on, comparing stories of Ytre Arna with reports from the capital. Unghird bullying and the dreadful treatment of Jews were patterns Lise had often witnessed in Oslo where the Jewish population was much larger.

Changes in school studies and bans on Norwegian culture were familiar, too. Nazis had ordered drastic changes in University courses, and the library collection was gutted. Lise reported increasing arrests of suspected resistance fighters, filling the notorious Grini Prison.

One bit of Mari's news managed to impress Lise.

"What a clever idea for Mrs. Tomasson and Astrid to move in with Mrs. Nilsson." Lise clapped her approval. "It's a perfect arrangement!"

"Mrs. Nilsson came up with the idea," Mari said. "So Astrid and her mother turned their little flat in town over to the German soldiers. Mrs. Nilsson's arthritis was getting worse and she needed help around the house. 'There's no medicine better than good company,' she says. She loves having them there, and she's crazy about Thor, too. Her old cat Alf wasn't happy about the arrangement at first, but he made peace with Thor once he established who was boss."

Lise chuckled and pushed her left sleeve above her wrist. She angled her arm toward Mari and said, "It's lucky for Thor that Alf befriended him. I still have scars from his scratches!"

Mari examined the faint traces on her sister's forearm. "Really? He's enormous now, but such a cuddly fellow. He's as warm as a furnace when he sits on my lap."

Lise nodded. "I was about your age when Alf was a kitten. Between Mama and Bestemor, I almost never got to hold you as a baby. When I tried to swaddle Alf instead, he didn't appreciate the idea."

Mari laughed. "Mrs. Nilsson says Alf thinks being a Norwegian Forest Cat means he's the king of the jungle. He looks more like a fuzzy monkey to me. He's quite the hunter, though. Astrid says if they were willing to eat rodents, Alf would supply enough for all of them to dine like kings."

Lise laughed. "I remember that. The first time her sons were home from sea and met Alf, they wanted to take him aboard their boat to keep it clear of vermin. Mrs. Nilsson wouldn't hear of it."

Then her light tone shifted to a more solemn one. "I'm glad their new living arrangements are working out, because they could be together a long time. After Pearl Harbor was bombed and America joined the war effort, we hoped the Allies could push Hitler back into Germany. But the Nazi broadcasts and newspapers insist we shouldn't 'worry' because Hitler will defend his 'German Fortress in the North' at all costs. Everyone says even more troops will be coming."

She patted Mari's hand. "Alf, Thor, and the rest of us must make room for them, I'm afraid."

Mari was anxious to ask Lise about Leif, but their parents would return soon. Her questions would wait until bedtime.

Chapter Eighteen

Laughter and Longing

Lise's suitcase treasures included two wedges of cheese, a large sausage, a half-kilo of butter, and three kilos of *real* flour. She even brought two fresh eggs, wrapped and tucked into small jars. No wonder the case had been so heavy.

Lise begged them to save everything for Jul dinner, since she'd have treats at the farm with Erik's family. Mama overruled her, insisting on having some of the luxuries that night as a family holiday celebration. Papa took Lise to the garage to retrieve the waffle pan so Bestemor and Mama could prepare a modest smorgasbord. Mari spread a crisp tablecloth and set the kettle to boil, picturing Lise's face when Papa revealed his secret.

The crowded kitchen percolated with voices more relaxed and joyous than Mari had heard in many long months. This precious family time was a gift indeed. She laughed with the others when Bestemor commented, "At least the Germans won't be intruding on our celebrations like last year. There's barely room for one of them to squeeze a boot in the door!"

Last Jul seemed like more than just a year ago, and yet the memory of it left a sour taste in Mari's mouth. Knowing now that it had been a ruse to choose suitable housing for soldiers was an even greater insult.

The cottage was crowded, but being together there was far better than living in the same house with the soldiers. Leif's accusation came to mind: Many villagers were worse off than her family.

Since graduating as a nurse last spring, Lise was working at the University Hospital. During their short holiday break she and Erik had traveled first to his parents' farm in the midlands. Lise would return to be with them for Jul, which was a full week away, but her visit to Ytre Arna meant Mari's Christmas wish came true.

Mari couldn't take her eyes off of her sister at dinner. Rationing had slimmed Lise dramatically, making her petite stature and delicate features look fragile. Mari had so much more to tell and ask, privately, but it would wait. For now, the family celebrated in Bestemor's tiny kitchen, hanging onto Lise's every word.

When Lise complimented her younger sister's willowy figure, Mari shook her head and changed the subject. She felt awkward and unattractive, all knobby knees and jutting angles. She would trade every mouthful of holiday treats for just an ounce of Lise's grace and confidence.

Her sister leaned in, keeping her voice low. Mari and

the others did the same, their heads nearly touching over the tabletop. "Erik really wanted to come with me, but when we arrived at his homestead there was far more work to do than he expected."

Her sister's new husband was an engineer in Oslo. "He planned to help his father convert farm machinery and trucks to wood-burning engines. All fieldwork is done with horses now, since gasoline and diesel are no longer available. Keeping the farm producing to the levels demanded by German quotas is exhausting. Erik's father hadn't even begun the conversions."

Mama had been holding Lise's hands since the meal ended. "Are his parents staying well? They aren't young, and their farm helpers probably took off for the mountains."

Lise nodded sadly. "One couple nearby helps out when they can. They're not young either, but they pitch in on the bigger projects, and Erik's parents share their reserves with them. The weather this year was good so they met German quotas, stored their official allowances, and managed to hide away extras for bartering. That's why they were able to send a few things to help you celebrate Jul. They wished it could have been more, but they send it with their love."

Never had holiday foods tasted as welcome or as luscious. They spent hours at the table, sharing news and singing Jul songs. Bestemor reluctantly signaled an end to their festivities. "I'd sit here all night with you if I could, sweet angel, but my eyes won't stay open any longer."

Papa gave her a hand up while Mama arranged a nest of bedding and pillows on the sofa. Bestemor gave Lise a lingering goodnight hug. Then Mari and Lise dimmed the lights and cleared away dishes as quietly as possible. Lise wiped the table, placed the last of the cups on the counter, and stretched up to Mari's ear to whisper, "Let's wash these in the morning so they can get to sleep."

Mari was startled to realize she was taller than her adult sister. She wasn't yet thirteen years old but she had outgrown the three generations of women she most admired.

After Lise took a turn, Mari went into the washroom and wiped her face. Instead of brushing her teeth she rinsed her mouth with clear water, savoring remnants of holiday flavors on her tongue as long as possible. The past year and a half had matured her, but her reflection in the mirror grinned back impishly at this childish self-indulgence.

With Mama and Papa settled behind their curtain and Bestemor already snoring softly, Mari opened the door to the bedroom. "Lise?" she whispered into the darkness.

Silence was the only answer.

She slipped into the room, clicked the door shut, and sat on her bed. "Lise, I need to talk to you about something important."

The silence wasn't absolute. Lise's steady breathing, in and out, in and out, signaled that questions would wait yet another day.

Chapter Nineteen

Attic Secrets

Working together the next morning the sisters plowed through heaps of dirty clothing and linens. When the last of the wet sheets were hanging on the network of ropes strung throughout the cellar of the main house, Mari confirmed that all eleven soldiers had left for the village. Row upon row of clean sheets and long underwear crisscrossed the cellar, and dripping water circled the drain.

"Let's get back to the cottage," Mari said, tugging Lise's hand. "I need to ask you some questions."

Within minutes they were at the table, warming their chapped fingers around steaming cups of tea. Lise asked, "What's so important, little one?"

Mari was suddenly tongue-tied.

"Is Mama or Papa ill? I was shocked at the changes in them in less than a year. Their hair is as gray as Bestemor's, and they're both too thin. You are, too."

Before Mari could answer Lise continued, "I'm surprised at how well Bestemor is doing. The arthritis in her hips and knees actually seems better with less weight to carry around."

Lise's question caused Mari a sudden wave of guilt. "Do *you* think they're ill? They seem so strong to me, no matter how hard things get. I should do more of the work. Especially for Bestemor."

Lise patted Mari's hand. "Nei, everyone's doing as well as possible. But it was a shock to see the changes after such a short time. Are *you* well? You're so tall, and still growing. You already do more than you should at your age." She gestured toward the baskets of clean laundry. "The ironing can wait. So, what *do* you need to talk about?"

Mari wasn't sure where to start. Instead she said, "I've got something to show you. Follow me."

As soon as Mari set foot on the bottom rung of the ladder, Lise clapped and giggled. "The attic? I love Bestemor's attic!"

In minutes they were seated near the trunk. Lise was staring from wall to wall, craning her neck to see beyond the stone chimney. Mari pushed the notebook into her hands.

"Wha—?"

"Just read it, please." Mari said.

Lise skimmed it, front to back, then read a few pages. "This is to Bjorn. Do you want me to get it to him?"

Her question stunned Mari. "Could you? Can your

contacts do that?"

Lise draped an arm around Mari's waist. "Nei, little one. No one is ever sure where he is. If we tried, the risk to everyone involved would be too great. It's not possible."

A floodgate of fears opened. Between sniffles Mari explained all about Bjorn's request, the ledger Per was keeping, and the letters she had been writing to their brother.

"I carried it around with me because, even though we keep the cottage locked all the time, I have this fear that the soldiers might search the cottage when we're away. I'm terrified they'll find the radio in Bestemor's bedroom, too."

Lise hugged the notebook to her chest, as Mari had often done. "Do Mama and Papa know about this?"

"I started to tell them, but never did. When safe talk is possible, they have more important things to say. Keeping this notebook is a small thing. But it's important to me. So I was desperate for a place to write and hide this."

Lise scanned the attic again. "This is a smart choice, Mari."

Mari nodded and took the notebook, slipping it into the trunk. "I'm counting on that. Because if they decide to search here, it will be easy to find. At least it's safer than carrying it around in my backpack."

Lise brushed a stray cobweb from her shoulders. "I had forgotten how low the ceiling is. When Bjorn and I were small, we spent long winter laundry days up here while Mama and Bestemor ironed."

She crawled on her hands and knees the length of the

attic, pausing here and there to lift a lid of a box or pull open the drawer of a small chest.

She stopped suddenly to focus on a sturdy bookcase. "There it is. . . ." Lise mumbled.

Mari crawled behind her, straining to see what had captured her sister's attention. She spotted an opening in the low wall, one she didn't remember. "What is this? Where does it go?"

Lise just asked, "Does Papa have a flashlight downstairs? Can you get it?"

Mari nodded, and scurried off to climb down the wall ladder. In a few minutes they were exploring the cramped space half hidden by the case. Light from the windows didn't reach into this alcove, so Lise probed the darkest corners with the flashlight's beam while she explained. "This is the portion of the attic that extends out over the furnace room beyond the kitchen."

It, too, had wooden floors and a heavy beam ceiling, but in this section the roof dropped all the way to the floor at the outer edges, leaving very little room to move about.

"How did I miss this?" Mari said. "And why is it so much colder in here?" She pressed one hand onto the floorboards and with the other she brushed frost from an overhead beam.

Lise did the same. "The floors absorb some warmth from below, but we're in the shadow of the mountain on this side of the cottage, where the sun never reaches, and winter snow gathers and clings to the slate tiles far into spring." She looked out into the open attic and back into the alcove. "Hmm, It's colder than I remember."

Mari couldn't remember playing in that dark space and couldn't imagine why anyone would want to.

"In my memory this was much larger." Lise crawled back out of the space, leaning against the chimney to brush off her skirt. "When Bjorn and I played hide and seek he could squeeze himself into the tiniest crevices in there. I'd like to see him try it now!"

Mari joined her and they worked their way to the hatch.

"Wait!" Lise said. "I have an idea. Give me your notebook."

Mari pulled it from the trunk and watched her sister return to the center of the garret. Instead of stopping, she continued on several feet to a small boxy stool, topped with a worn thick cushion with a tapestry cover.

"Watch this," Lise said. She wiggled and jiggled the top until it lifted off, revealing a cavity with knitting supplies inside. One slot had a skein and several balls of yarn. A small ledge held long needles and crochet hooks, and another space seemed intended for unfinished projects. Lise grinned, then clicked the divider between the spaces, and it popped open to reveal a magazine and several knitting patterns. She separated the papers, dropped in the notebook, and clicked it shut again.

"Ta-da! Hocus-pocus, your sister is a genius. Even if someone comes here they'll never imagine something is in there. And I don't think the soldiers are too interested in knitting."

Mari traded places with Lise, examining the stool with the cushioned top. It was a perfect place to hide a small notebook. Meanwhile, Lise continued sweeping the light around the attic.

Suddenly she stooped and pulled a cigar box from a dark corner. "Look at this." Lise set the box on the floor under the flashlight's beam. Across the top, written in crayon with childish block letters was written: *SKATT.*

Treasure. Mari and Lise exchanged grins and lifted the lid.

It contained Bjorn's childhood collection of miniature metal cars, the paint mostly worn bare from hours of play. Mari unrolled a handkerchief holding a delicate wooden ark with three pairs of tiny animals.

Lise removed a fist-sized chunk of wood, turning it over and over, then pressing it to her heart. "I remember this. Bjorn learned to carve figures from grandfather, and this was one of the first things Bjorn made that actually looked like anything." She handed it to Mari. "See? You can tell it's supposed to be a bear. He was just six or seven when he made this. Bestefar died soon after."

Mari held it, then nestled it into the box with the other toys. "I wonder if he even remembers it's here."

Lise closed the box and settled it onto the lowest shelf of the heavy bookcase.

With a silent look they agreed it was time to return to

the kitchen.

After their feet were firmly on the pantry floor with the ladder door latched, Mari laughed.

"What?"

She pointed to the bathroom and said, "Go see for yourself." The sight of her pretty sister's face streaked with dust and spider webs was only one source of Mari's happy amusement. For the first time in months she felt at ease.

Several minutes later, they were both clean and sipping mint tea at the table. They still had the cottage all to themselves.

Mari talked more about what a burden it had been to keep the notebook a secret. Lise wasn't sure that was a good idea. In fact, she felt strongly that Mari should tell Mama, Papa, and Bestemor she was using the attic.

Mari asked about ideas for ways to code the information in the notebook. She stood up to reheat the water for more tea, bumping her chair against the wall. "I try to write in a way that wouldn't get me or the family in trouble if a German soldier got his hands on my notes. But I can't write about what I see and feel without being honest. And that could be a problem. Is there a way to hide my anger? Or the truth about what's happening here? Answers come easily to me in school, but I can't figure out a way to write things safely!"

Lise sighed. "There's a reason for that, Mari."

Mari gripped the kettle and stared at her sister.

Lise continued, "There *is* no safe way to write about

what the occupation is doing to us."

Mari spun away from the stove. "How can you say that? I can't let Bjorn down! I know what trouble I'd be in, we could *all* be in . . . well, I don't know, and I don't *want* to know!"

She squeezed her eyes shut, took a deep breath, and released it slowly. When she opened her eyes her voice was steady. "Even so, I'll just have to take my chances. Bjorn is doing that, so I will, too!"

Lise got up and wrapped Mari in her arms, hugging her close. "During these times there aren't a lot of safe answers for loyal Norwegians. You knew it all along, I think, but you had to admit it to yourself." She leaned back and looked up into Mari's eyes.

"For someone not yet thirteen years old, you're so grown up and already one of the bravest people I know. I'm proud of you."

Mari returned her sister's hug and held on for a long time.

Lise's words reminded Mari of Leif's accusations. It was time to ask her sister's advice about him.

Chapter Twenty

Friend or Foe?

Over several more cups of tea Mari described her confusion about Leif. She started with the day he appeared at the pier and went right up to the encounter just a few weeks ago when he challenged her to "grow up" and make choices he called "smarter" ones.

There must be some way to understand why her classmate had turned his back on King Haakon VII and everything her family held dear. Could he be pretending? If she were better at disguising her real feelings maybe she could do that, too. Is that what Leif was suggesting? She was terrible at pretending, and wouldn't want to anyway.

To Mari's surprise, Lise had faced the same dilemmas many times in Oslo, only worse. Lise handed Mari a plate to dry and put away. "I've seen the way the German soldiers flirt or even bully pretty girls to spend time with them. Some feel they have no choice but to join NS because they're desperate for food or medicine."

Even wearing her wedding band, Lise said, wasn't always enough to deflect unwanted attention. For once,

Mari was grateful to be gawky and plain, but wondered how soon her pretty friends Astrid and Greta would be pressured to join Unghird.

They hung the dishtowels to dry and settled on the sofa. Mari peppered Lise with questions she hesitated to ask Mama, Papa, or even Bestemor. Leif's words had stung, and yet she'd been weighing their truth since she first heard them.

Providing the soldiers with comfortable accommodations made it easy for them to spend their days scouring the mountainside, trying to locate spies and evidence of resistance. The ration tickets earned and leftovers from the meals served to the soldiers meant they lived better than many in town. Did that make their family as bad as NS members?

Lise took her sister's hand and shifted so she could look into her eyes. "Little one, the only truth in Leif's words is that nothing is ever clearly black or white, good or bad. That's a harsh reality, no matter what your age. Remember, if Papa refused to cooperate, he'd be in jail. And soldiers would be sleeping in our house anyway."

Mari had come to that conclusion herself. Still, it felt wrong to do anything to help them.

"I have no doubt Mama overhears many things working in the house near the soldiers, just as Papa does running the trains. When people are most relaxed, their guard drops. Hosting those soldiers means they gain valuable information for the resistance."

Mari had considered that, too. But the reality of helping Hitler fit her conscience as uncomfortably as her outgrown clothes fit her body. "You're not saying we should all cooperate and pretend to agree with their sickening propaganda, are you?"

"Nei, of course not. But the question I ask myself is whether the actions I take are for the greater good. If they will improve someone else's life, not mine. Plenty are choosing to act in ways that favor themselves. But others take risks—"

"Like Bjorn!" Mari interrupted.

"Exactly. But some risks are less obvious. As an engineer, Erik has been chosen to help build airfields and anti-aircraft bunkers. If he doesn't, someone else will. Still, he says he won't contribute to helping the Germans cling to a land they've stolen."

Mari saw the pain in Lise's face and tried to picture Erik thrown into Grini prison for refusing to help. Her sister's pride in the man she loved was obvious.

Mari felt a twist of guilt. She idolized her brother Bjorn for his brave choice to join the mountain fighters, but overlooked the courage of those who stayed behind, like Erik, only to be confronted with hard choices.

"Can't Erik join the fighters, too?" To herself, Mari thought if he did, Lise might come back home to live.

"Nei, Mari. He believes they would punish *me* if he disappeared."

Mari gasped at a possibility she hadn't considered. Leif

was right about one thing: she really did need to grow up.

Lise got up to refill their cups. "We've worked out a way that might solve the situation, if we're lucky."

Mari swung around. "What? What are you planning?"

"Something we've tried often works. The Germans are absolute fanatics when it comes to cleanliness and avoiding disease. Especially *contagious* ones."

Mari laughed, holding out her dry, cracked hands. "I know exactly what you mean. I've done enough laundry to destroy every germ in Ytre Arna!"

Lise continued. "When we return to Oslo, I'll start giving Erik medications that will cause him to be nauseous. He'll have diarrhea and lose weight. He'll be miserable, but we can make a convincing case that he has a dangerous stomach infection. When it doesn't clear up, he'll ask to be sent to stay with his parents on their farm until he can recover—to avoid contaminating the others working on those airfield projects."

Mari felt a wave of relief. "My sister *is* a genius, truly you are!"

Now it was Lise's turn to laugh. "Not really. We're just learning to use the enemy's own fears and patterns against them. That's another reason to balance our disgust for the Nazi invaders with careful observation. I don't agree with Leif that you should pretend to be his friend just to feel safer. But it won't help you or our cause if you antagonize him. Does that make any sense?"

"I suppose it does, but where do I draw the line? How

do I figure it out?" Mari sighed.

"Let's hope this occupation is over before you need all the answers. For now, you need to talk more with Mama, Papa, and Bestemor. They should know about your using the attic, about your fears and worries. We're all stronger when we share our burdens."

Mari knew she was right. "I will, I promise."

Lise carried her cup to the hearth, kneeling near the fire's blaze. "It's always colder in Oslo than on the coast, but this winter has been brutal everywhere." Mari joined her, wrapping an arm around Lise's waist and leaning her head on her sister's shoulder.

Lise added, "Just remember that even the worst winter is followed by spring. Though you can't feel it coming, it's inevitable. Don't ever give up hope."

The sound of steps on the porch, followed by the click of the lock, meant that Bestemor and Mama were returning to the cottage for a rest before making dinner for the soldiers. When they got settled in, Mari and Lise prepared a bit of a tea party for the four of them from the scraps of the previous night's celebration.

Mama lifted her cup in a toast. "To my two beautiful daughters." They all raised their cups and sipped. "Did you have a chance for some special girl talk while you worked on the laundry?"

"Ja, Mama," they replied in unison.

In the midst of their laughter, Lise caught Mari's eye and winked.

Chapter Twenty-One

Dear Bjorn

Winter, 1942

The week after Christmas most of the soldiers were on leave, so Mari found time to talk to Mama Papa, and Bestemor about her worries.

"We won't have all the answers, little one, but we're always here to help," Mama promised.

Bestemor gave Mama a gentle poke. "Speak for yourself, Sonja. I'm never short of answers!"

When it came to Leif, they were in agreement that Mari should ignore his accusations.

"It's to our advantage for NS members to think we sympathize," Papa explained. "Or at least to say we're not taking sides. Our real friends know us, and Nazi supporters will see us as less of a threat."

He patted Mari's hands and pulled his chair closer. "Lise was right. As the soldiers relax their guard in conversations and watchfulness, the less they concern themselves with us."

Bestemor added, "Like others, we've been sharing our extra ration tickets with the weakest elders and the smallest children in the village."

Mari nodded. She was beginning to understand.

Mari told them next about Bjorn's request to Per to keep some notes about what was happening in the village. Papa thought it was a wise idea, one that could help Per gain perspective on the occupation and the resistance. As for her own notebook, the letters to Bjorn she could never send, Mari simply said that she was keeping a journal to write about her confusions and worries, and that Lise helped her find a place to hide it in the attic.

Her parents agreed it made sense as long as she spent as little time up there as possible. They asked her to limit her writing to times when one of them was home so that unexpected visitors could be delayed, allowing Mari time to scramble down from the attic. And they insisted that she use no lights. Adding blackout curtains now would be noticed and prompt a search, so writing during daylight hours was her only option. With short winter days she had only a few hours available in the mornings before leaving for school in the afternoons.

They discussed allowing her to write at the kitchen table now and then. If someone came to the door, they would identify a quick spot to hide the journal. But Mari had begun to feel safe in the attic—truly alone with her deepest thoughts. She would continue writing there.

In fact, Mari resolved to start writing to Bjorn *from her heart* on New Year's Day. Papa would be home for part of the day, and there was no laundry to do. She wrote several pages about Lise's visit.

She found herself looking forward to writing in the days to come: the exhilaration of slipping up the ladder, the quiet moments in her sheltered space to record the truth of local events that she had been thinking about, and the release of adding her own feelings and questions.

In the next days she spilled her thoughts out onto page after page, writing letters she could never send. For reasons she couldn't explain, just writing them made her feel better.

By mid-January she was writing each dated entry as freely as if she *could* drop the letters into an envelope and mail them to Bjorn with no fear of censors reading her words. For those few minutes in each day, she wrote to him as if he could hear her every word.

> January 14.
>
> Dear Bjorn,
>
> A new soldier arrived at the house recently. I call him Goatman. He's some kind of radio specialist. Mama says the other soldiers are counting on him to track down British agents hiding on the mountainside.

He's a strange man: not much older than you, but he's got a long narrow face and a scrawny gray-ish chin-beard. He mutters when he talks, then his chin wobbles side to side. He's as pushy as a goat too, showing up out of nowhere and for no reason at all.

Yesterday, after the squad of soldiers marched away into the village, I loaded a basket with sheets and shirts to iron back at the cottage. When I reached the top step, there he stood, as if he was waiting for me.

He took the laundry basket from me before I could stop him. I insisted I could manage and I even spoke in German! But he took the basket and crossed right over to the cottage door as if he didn't understand me. Then, before I could pull out my key, HE OPENED THE DOOR!

We always keep the cottage locked, even when one of us is inside. We thought that provided some privacy. But Goatman just turned the knob and walked in! Then he looked at me with his awful scrawny beard twitching back and forth as if he were chewing his cud.

I wracked my brain making sure I had locked the door. I remembered how cold the key felt when I had it out earlier for just the few minutes needed to lock up and then tucked it back inside my shirt.

That door WAS locked when I left for the cellar. I'm sure of it. Had he been in the cottage the whole time I was in the cellar working? We're never safe from their spying, and Goatman is the worst of the bunch.

I pushed past him and grabbed the basket, blocking the doorway. He muttered something I couldn't understand and backed off the stoop, his ugly chin twitching. I locked the door so fast I'm sure he heard it, but he just strolled across the yard and out the gate. I peeked out the window to see where he was going. He crossed the road to Mr. Meier's place and walked right in there, too.

I checked everything important in the cottage, especially in Bestemor's room. Nothing seemed out of place. I watched until he left Meier's house and headed into town. Then I checked the attic. Everything was safe there, too. But I was too upset to write anything then.

When I told the family. Mama and Papa didn't say much, but Papa went out and checked the lock right away. It seemed fine.

Mama checked to see if anything was taken or disturbed.

Bestemor just snorted and looked furious, like she wanted to storm over and give Goatman a piece of her mind. Or a good thumping.

If he's such an important expert, why is Goatman always on his own instead of working with the rest of the soldiers on patrol?

If you were here you'd find out what he's up to, I know it.

Take care, Bjorn. We all love you and hope to see you safely home soon.

January 17.

Dear Bjorn,

Mama and Bestemor report lots of news from the big house. All the soldiers talk about these days is tracking down spies, homegrown or from the Allies. A twelfth German moved into the house this week. His specialty is decoding radio transmissions they intercept.

Since I talked to them after Lise left, Mama, Papa, and Bestemor have been more open in their conversations when I'm around. Even if they wanted to shield me from details, there's no place they can send me! Sometimes I manage to surprise them with news I overhear at school.

The patrol marches into town some mornings, but most often they climb up into the mountains, hauling packs and equipment to track and record radio signals. For several months now, Leif has been tagging along whenever they allow it. When that happens, he wastes no time strutting and cawing his news like a crow.

I wish that boy didn't confuse me so much. Lise was right. I can't sort people into piles of "good" or "bad" as easily as I once did. But Leif is as close to the "bad" pile as anyone I know. I get so angry when he says how clever and wonderful the soldiers are. I want to kick him!

I hope you've found good people for company, people you can trust. Stay warm and safe, wherever you are on these bitterly cold and dark winter nights.

After dinner one evening Papa asked "That new soldier—I wonder if he's having any success tracking down radio signals?"

Mari spoke up. "This evening Leif followed me home from school to share a funny story. He said the squad captain was furious after their morning search.

"Since the new specialist arrived they've located more radio signals. Leif said they were certain they had zeroed in on a certain cottage that was hiding the transmitter. Today was the day they planned to raid it and capture the operator."

Papa leaned in, his brow furrowed under hair that was becoming grayer by the day. "Did he say whose cottage it was?"

"Leif just said it was on the other side of the village. He said he didn't recognize the place when they surrounded it. He was annoyed when they ordered him to stay back while they barged through the door. He heard loud screeching and then many women's voices yelling all at once."

Mari couldn't resist grinning at the worried faces surrounding her. "All they found was a sewing circle of old women. Leif claimed one was so frightened she nearly had a heart attack."

Mari saw Bestemor clutch the buttons of her dress, so she quickly added, "He said everyone was fine, eventually. The women were marched out and had to wait in the barn while soldiers searched the cottage from top to bottom. They found nothing. So they moved the women back to the house while the barn was searched. Again, nothing.

"When Leif left for school, he said the captain was ranting at the new man and Goatman, calling them idiots and bumblers."

Bestemor's chuckling sparked a round of laughter as they savored that image.

After school, Leif had insisted on walking Mari home, eager to describe every detail. At one point, he looked around to be sure they were alone, and then laughed about how foolish the Germans looked. Mari struggled to hide her enjoyment of the failed raid. He might have been trying to trick her.

Safe in her home, gathered at the table with her family, a good laugh felt long overdue. Mari was anxious to write about this for Bjorn. She could picture him reading over her shoulder with a wide grin.

"If that's the best they can do," Bestemor said, "let them keep searching for whoever is exchanging messages with England. We have no trouble getting the BBC reports almost every night, and I'm sure we're not under suspicion." She dabbed at the corners of her eyes and giggled again.

Papa nodded, but his smile had disappeared. "Thank goodness they raided the wrong place. Anyone captured or even suspected is taken in for questioning and faces Gestapo torture. German patience is short, and arrests are increasing daily around the region."

Mari felt tension grip her shoulders and clench her jaw at the thought of Papa or Bjorn in the hands of the Gestapo.

"What if the prisoners refuse to talk, Papa? Are they shot?"

Her question was barely a whisper, but in a kitchen gone suddenly still her words rang in her ears as if she had shouted.

"It happens, Mari. If they think there's information to be had, they try to keep the prisoner alive. Important prisoners are transferred to Grini Prison near Oslo."

Just the sound of the word *Grini* made Mari's heart leap into her throat. Lise had described treatment there as brutal, with diets near starvation, and reprisals carried out against the general population in Oslo if anyone dared to escape.

One spy they caught had been abused so badly they sent him to the hospital to speed his recovery—so they could resume his questioning. Lise had seen the results of their "questioning" with her own eyes. Lise didn't give many details, but Mari couldn't block out her imagination.

Ever since Mari heard about that, she imagined Bjorn being caught. Some nights she was jolted awake by nightmares of Bjorn, captured and suffering. Then she would lie awake for hours, wondering where he was, if he was safe. She dreaded the thought that sometimes followed: it might be better for him to be killed fighting than to be captured.

Chapter Twenty-Two

Quisling Headaches

One evening after school, Mari waved good-bye to Astrid at Mrs. Nilsson's house and began the climb to Bestemor's cottage. A nightmare had robbed her of sleep the previous night. That, combined with an unexpected quiz in German history class, had her right temple throbbing in pain. Each crunch of stones on the road and piercing cry of a swooping gull made her headache worse. She rubbed the tender area near her hairline, eager to loosen her braid and lie down for a few minutes when she reached home.

Leif's voice made her flinch. She had no patience to put on an act.

"Wait until you hear the news, Mari!" He jogged toward her from the bottom of the hill.

She called back, "Not tonight, Leif. I'm not well." She lengthened her stride and increased her pace, but Leif easily caught up.

"I'm sorry you're ill, Mari, but you'll want to know about this." He tugged the strap of her pack and spun her around. His usual smug expression shifted to one of concern, and his hand dropped to her arm. "Oh, what's wrong? Should I get your mother?"

Mari winced at the pain in her head and tugged loose of his grip. "NEI! Just leave me alone!"

Leif took a step back, startled. After a moment, he flipped his pack open, dug through a stack of newspapers, and shoved one into her hands. His arrogant expression was back, and he spoke with sarcastic exaggeration.

"Please, forgive my intrusion, *Fräulein*. My mistake to think you'd want an early copy of tomorrow's newspaper."

He nodded toward the paper clutched in her fist. "We aren't supposed to deliver these until morning but I thought I'd do *my friends* a favor. Changes are coming. Soon. Read this tonight. Your whole family should consider carefully who your friends *really* are."

He glared at her, waiting for a response.

Mari glared right back, but she gripped the paper, desperate to know more about his news.

After a few moments in a standoff, Leif turned on his heel and jogged across the road to Mr. Meier's house where his aunt was watching at the door. "Big news, *Tante* Helene!"

Mari told herself she'd let her head split in two before she'd allow Leif or the soldiers smoking in the garden to see her cry. She hurried through the gate and rushed past a blur of German uniforms. Once inside the cottage, she collapsed onto the sofa in pain.

When Mari woke her mouth was as gritty as beach sand. Someone had covered her and tucked a pillow under her head while she slept. She licked her lips and rubbed away the crusty residue that sealed her eyes.

With tentative fingers she massaged her temple and breathed a sigh of relief at the absence of pain. In fact, other than a slightly stiff neck, she felt more rested and relaxed than she had in weeks.

In the dark parlor she gathered the pillow and quilt from the sofa. As she tiptoed toward the bedroom, she noticed the newspaper spread open on the kitchen table. The memory of Leif's warning and his hateful glare stopped her in her tracks, and she dropped the bedding back on the sofa. Within a step of the kitchen, a hand caught her arm and pulled her back.

"Sit here, little one. I'll tell you the news." Bestemor gestured to the footstool in front of her chair.

Mari hadn't realized her grandma was in the darkened room. She saw that Bestemor, too, had a pillow and quilt folded next to her chair.

"Bestemor, you should be in bed. Let's go, we'll talk about the news in the morning." Mari tugged her grandma to her feet.

Bestemor laughed and pulled Mari into a hug. "It *is* morning! Lift the blackout curtains and you'll see."

They tied up the heavy window coverings and sun streamed in, making Mari squint until her eyes adjusted to the light.

"Sonja fed the soldiers without my help this morning so I could sit with you until you woke. How does your head feel today?" She wrapped one arm around Mari's waist and led her to the table.

Bestemor filled the kettle and set it on the stove to heat.

Mari touched her temple gingerly, half expecting the throbbing to resume. "I never had such a headache before, but a good night's sleep erased it completely."

When the kettle whistled, Bestemor poured two cups of tea, then stood behind Mari and gently massaged her shoulders and neck. "Sip your tea, little one, and slow your breathing. Don't let Quisling and the Germans devour you from the inside the way they are swallowing Norway."

That day's laundry would wait. The two sat for several hours discussing the notices in the paper. Quisling was the Norwegian traitor, the government leader who had "invited" the Germans into the country in the early days and helped make the invasion in April possible two years ago. He saw it as his path to power.

To his dismay, the Germans allowed him very little authority. As the leader of NS, he was just a figurehead, a puppet. Quisling was often the butt of resistance jokes and cartoons in the Jossing papers.

After America entered the war, Quisling convinced Hitler that with more power, he could get his countrymen to support the Germans. Hitler agreed, and immediately Quisling imposed laws that increased fines, imprisonment, and stricter enforcement of rules. Leif's newspaper was filled with the latest new directives.

At school that afternoon, Mari's mind buzzed with the new pressures that overwhelmed her life. In the days that followed, she fought off headaches with Mrs. Nilsson's herbal teas and Bestemor's massages. Quisling's new rules and consequences were issued faster than her letters to Bjorn could keep up.

Chapter Twenty-Three

Demanding Change

January 24.

Dearest Brother,

Quisling's latest dictate is that everyone must "volunteer" more supplies to fight the Russians. They demand blankets, coats, sweaters, boots, and more. Papa provided three mattresses, bags of clothing, and some tools. The Germans seem satisfied and thanked him for supporting Hitler's cause!

Coins are no longer used for purchases. They must be exchanged for paper currency. Then, our metal coins are melted down to make weapons and ammunition.

Papa hid as many coins as he can spare, but we have so little money as it is. Thank goodness the gold bullion from the Norwegian treasury was taken to England when King Haakon escaped. If not, they might use it to make gold bullets.

Our men and teenage boys face mounting pressure to join the German army. Leif insists if he were old enough he'd join now! I can hardly believe the words as they leave his mouth, which they seem to do every time I see him.

The Germans live in our homes and gobble up our food. Then they send our fathers and brothers as "volunteers" to fight on the Russian battlefields. Papa says those troops are likely to be killed within days of their arrival.

How can Leif be so stupid not to see that? He often infuriates me, but I wouldn't want him to die in battle.

February 3.

I don't understand, Bjorn. How can Quisling expect us to comply with decrees for new rules and laws daily? He gained full power barely a week ago, but ridiculous demands come faster than we can keep up.

He insists Norwegians will finally adopt "New Norway" culture and give up our old ways. The effects are the opposite—they only make us more sure of who we really are.

Wearing ANY red clothing, especially red

knit caps, is now officially a crime! Can you believe it? Violators are subject to arrest. Any red clothing makes you an enemy of the Third Reich.

Public dancing and singing are illegal now, too. Except, of course, when celebrating Germany. Concerts and public performances require advance approval of their programs and can't include any traditional Norwegian stories or music. How are children like the Molstads' son supposed to learn about their true heritage?

You should see little Johan, Bjorn. He's such a clever boy, but he hasn't been well lately. In a small act of decency, children under six years are allowed more milk than the few dribbles permitted to the rest of us. Until this winter Johan seemed to be growing well, but for more than a month he's been fighting a terrible cough of some kind. Doctor Olsen seems baffled by it, and the Molstads are worried sick.

Are you well, Bjorn? You're resourceful, I know, but I worry about how you're doing. Oh, how I wish I knew.

February 4.

Have you heard, Bjorn? Quisling declared this month a national period of mourning for the loss of German lives in Russia. It's good news, in a way. Hitler's early success there is over. BBC estimates German losses in fierce fighting at 150,000 killed, 90,000 prisoners, and countless wounded. It was surprising to hear those numbers confirmed in Fritt Folk, since they never admit to setbacks.

Memorial ceremonies are scheduled once a week. We are supposed to praise Germany's soldiers, sing German songs, and listen to recruitment speeches. It turns my stomach, but at least they're no longer winning in Russia.

A secret group of resistance fighters was discovered in Ålesund on the coast. Quisling ordered executions of everyone involved. No names were printed this time, but Papa says it couldn't be anyone we know.

I hope you are safe, Bjorn.

February 5.

Quisling has lost his mind, Bjorn! He ordered all teachers to join the new NS Teachers Union. They must sign papers of loyalty, supporting "New Norway," NS, and Hitler. They're ordered what to teach, including all the German propaganda.

Many labor groups, doctors, engineers, and lawyers are facing the same requirements.

Unless they give in they will lose their jobs.

Quisling ordered that EVERY boy and girl aged ten to eighteen must join their new Nazi youth force, the NSUF. It's like Unghird, only now it will include all children in Norway after their tenth birthday. It's as if the new Unghird Force will be a children's army for Hitler!

Mama and Papa talk about this every day, but haven't told me what they plan to do. What can they do if it's the law?

I was happy to be the youngest in my class, not turning thirteen until next month. I thought I'd have an extra year before being pushed to join Unghird. Maybe the war would end by then. But now?

If you knew this would happen, would you still have said I was stronger than I think? How am I supposed to fight rules like this?

I listen and imagine what you'd tell me, Bjorn, but all I hear is a threatening buzz in my mind, then the headaches return.

Chapter Twenty-Four

Taking a Stand

February, 1942

Papa crushed dried raspberry leaves into the bowl of his pipe and lit it. He sucked at the stem until embers glowed, his cheeks sinking with each deep, slow breath.

Mari studied his weathered and drawn features as she watched and waited, fingering the edge of the tablecloth. She examined Mama's and Bestemor's faces, too. Nearly two years of occupation and deprivation had aged them dramatically.

Tonight that seemed even more pronounced than usual.

Bestemor waved her hand in front of her nose, then used her apron to aim the smoke back toward Papa. "Are you smoking stinkweed these days, Anders? If we could blow that smell into the main house, the soldiers would evacuate."

"If an entire village farting every day hasn't forced the Germans out of Ytre Arna, my pipe smoke doesn't stand a chance."

They may have changed outwardly, but their robust laughter reassured Mari that her family was still the same in important ways.

Mama patted Papa's shoulder. "Don't begrudge him whatever he can find to stuff in that pipe. At the rate our paper currency is losing value, he may decide to try burning *kroner* next."

Papa's eyebrows rose, and his mustache twitched above his smile.

Bestemor added steaming water to their cups and scolded Mama. "Don't give him ideas, Sonja, he's devilish enough without suggestions like that." She pulled out her chair and settled into their tight little circle around the table. "Let's get down to business. My bones say I should have been in bed by now."

Mama turned to Mari. "Yes, we have important plans to discuss."

Mari sensed what was coming. Quisling's deadline for parents, teachers and labor groups to join unions, sign agreements, and enroll younger children in the Unghird Force was approaching. Time was running out. She had been praying that this wretched occupation would be over before she was fourteen, but now she was swept into the new decree.

Mama continued. "Beginning Monday, Quisling will

close all schools for a month or more, using the fuel shortages as an excuse."

This was surprising news to Mari.

"Ja, Mari, it's true. All across Norway, schools will close indefinitely. Students weren't told about it today because the papers will release the announcement Sunday."

An avalanche of emotions swept over Mari. The first wave was relief. She welcomed the reprieve from daily confrontations with German culture and history classes, propaganda, and Unghird bullying. But concern quickly followed. She wondered what would happen to her teachers, most of whom she admired and enjoyed.

Two years ago, in April 1940, Norwegian schools had closed soon after the German invasion. But classes resumed in the fall, and they had managed to get back on track with their studies. Would it be as easy to catch up, now that she was taking advanced science and math in Upper School? Before her mind could race on to other worries, Mama continued.

"The teachers refused to join the Nazi Union. So Quisling is just trying to save face for now."

"For now?" Mari pleaded for answers, "Quisling will have to reopen the schools, won't he?"

Papa patted her shoulder. "There's a lot to think about, Mari. Your mother and I have been talking."

Mari recognized the gritty intensity in Papa's eyes that signaled a stance as firmly anchored as the Trollheimen Mountains to the north. "Quisling and the Nazis have gone too far this time. The other parents feel the same. Teachers and church leaders helped our parent association draft a letter, refusing to allow our children to join Quisling's NSUF. Nearly every family will send the same letter, saying the same thing. You should read ours."

Papa unbuttoned his vest, slid his fingers into the lining, and removed a folded paper. He laid it on the table and smoothed it flat before nudging it toward Mari.

She looked from face to face to face, then began to read. It was a simple letter, addressed to President Quisling. It said that as parents, they and only they had the duty to ensure the safety and education of their child, Mari. They refused to allow her to join the NSUF, and they claimed full responsibility for her growth and education. It was only three sentences, closing with respect and both Mama's and Papa's full names and their address.

"Nei, nei!" She tried to stand but her chair bumped against the wall in the cramped kitchen. "You'll both be arrested!"

"Shhh, Mari, keep your voice down." Mama spoke her warning directly into Mari's ear, pressing a finger across her lips.

Papa stood and walked to the door, pipe in hand. He paused, looking back toward the now-silent table, before turning the key. He stepped outside. The door clicked shut after him.

In a few moments it reopened and he returned, locking the door behind him. Mari released the breath she didn't realize she'd been holding since he left. He set his empty pipe on the mantel and returned to the table.

"No soldiers in the garden tonight, but you've got to remember to keep your voice down, Mari. The thick walls of this old cottage allow us some privacy, but you never know when a soldier might be out there having a smoke or just enjoying the night air. We have a curfew, but they don't."

Mari struggled to speak softly, but her words tumbled out. "You can't do this. Let me join. I will say or do whatever they require. It won't change me, I promise. I need you both here at home with me. Please don't do this!"

Her voice was escalating as she spoke, in spite of her best intentions. She covered her mouth with one shaking hand and choked back any further protests.

Her parents exchanged a long look. Papa nudged his chair closer and wrapped his long arm around Mari's shoulders, pulling her head to his chest. He kissed her forehead before speaking.

"The truth is, we *could* be arrested. But if we are, many thousands of other parents will be arrested, too. This is exactly the same letter that nearly every parent in Norway will deliver on Sunday afternoon.

"The tradespeople and the church ministers will all deliver their refusals the same afternoon, too. I'll hand in a second letter, refusing to join the train workers' Nazi union. So they'll have double reason to arrest me."

He smiled wryly. "But they won't. Even with all the

forces Hitler has stationed here, how could they actually arrest us all? And if everyone was in jail, who will run this country they are stealing? Who will grow their food, operate their trains and buses, serve in their stores and businesses and banks?

"Believe me, Mari, we don't want to be arrested. But we don't believe that will happen."

Mari struggled to grasp what he had said.

Hundred of thousands of letters, all delivered the same day? All across the country? All refusing to follow Quisling's orders?

"How can you be sure the others will do the same?" she argued. "What if they are too frightened, or decide to do as Leif said and choose the Nazis for friends?" She sat up and sought her father's eyes. Seeing his granite strength and certainty would ease her heart and allow her to believe.

Instead his elbows were propped on the table, his forehead resting on his folded hands, his eyes closed.

She looked to Mama, then to Bestemor, and both had done the same—lowered their heads and closed their eyes.

For several moments she did, too. But unlike them, she couldn't claim to be praying, or even making a wish. No, she was hiding, pulling the blackout curtains of her eyelids down and cowering behind them, unwilling to admit what was waiting when she opened them again.

Chapter Twenty-Five

New Challenges

When Mari came to the table the next morning, her grandma poured steaming water into a cup and pulled out a chair. "Good morning, little one, how are you feeling?" She crumbled mint leaves into the cup and set it before her granddaughter.

Mari inhaled the brew and blew on it for a few moments before she sipped. Today, even more than most days, she longed for a sprinkle of sugar or a dribble of cream. Just a hint of comfort, of normalcy. A cup of strong coffee would be even better, but that was as impossible as turning cod liver oil into butter.

She leaned over and kissed her grandma's cheek. "I'm fine. Did you sleep well?"

"I did, in part because I was exhausted. But I dreamed up something that might make last night's discussion easier to bear. Your parents and I discussed it this morning before you woke."

The look on Bestemor's face made Mari put down her cup and lean in closer. "What? You found a secret to end this miserable war? The Germans are going away?" Her comment was only a joke, but a flutter of hope nudged at her heart.

"Not yet. Give me a minute to work on that." Bestemor's index finger stroked her chin and she gazed at the ceiling as if pondering a math problem.

Mari twirled the liquid in her cup and tapped her toes on the table legs. "Tell me about your dream! What does it have to do with Quisling's rules?"

"Dreams sometimes help us fit together bits and pieces of our lives in new ways. Mine tied up threads of different conversations in a very clever way, if I do say so myself."

Bestemor leaned close. "Do you remember Lise telling us about Erik facing threats? How Erik was running out of excuses to refuse helping the Germans build military bases?"

Mari remembered Lise blinking back tears as she described how she was planning to use medicines to make Erik seem seriously ill, so he could leave his job in Oslo and help his parents on their farm. Lise had hinted that resistance workers knew other medical tricks to turn the Germans' fear of diseases against them. She was lost in her thoughts and missed what Bestemor said next.

Bestemor refilled their cups with steaming water. "We thought you'd want to do it, but if you are too frightened by the idea, no one will insist. I don't believe there will be arrests when the protest letters are filed, but if it happens, you and I will be fine here together until your Mama and Papa are released."

Mari winced at the mention of arrests. "Tell me what you've dreamed up for me to do, Bestemor."

For several minutes, Mari's grandmother described a proposal while Mari peppered her with questions.

Bestemor's idea was shocking—and intriguing. She proposed that Mari would work during the school closing as an assistant to Doctor Olsen; that she could learn some of Lise's tricks.

"But I'm still only twelve years old! Doctor Olsen won't agree to it. Lise has university training and knows how to keep people safe."

Bestemor patted her hand and chuckled. "Mari, when will you learn to believe in yourself as much as others believe in you?"

Mari considered the idea. The decision wasn't easy. But it offered her more choices than she had the night before. She liked the idea of spending time with the doctor and avoiding long days around Leif and a house full of German soldiers. But how dangerous were these tricks? What if she made mistakes? Lise said that the medications could actually harm Erik.

Bestemor continued, "Actually, my idea came from Doctor Olsen's request. Physicians were ordered to join Nazi unions like all the other professions. He's taking the train to Oslo later today to meet with colleagues about a resistance strategy. There will be more such trips. He mentioned he'll need someone to tend to his local patients while he's gone and asked if you would help."

A glow of pride filled Mari at the thought of Doctor Olsen's trust. She respected him greatly, and would never forget his gentle care for Bestemor and Odin when they needed medical attention. Mari was honored that he trusted her to care for his patients, even for a few days.

"But what if Mama and Papa *are* arrested? You can't take care of the house and the soldiers and the cottage by yourself. You need me here to help."

"No one will be arrested. If they haul everyone down to the police station, they'll just give them a fine and send them home. There's no room to keep more than a few people overnight in the cells."

Bestemor seemed so certain. Her confidence was the very thing Mari had hoped to find in Papa's eyes the night before.

"You'll have to decide quickly, though. Doctor Olsen is leaving this evening. If you're going to help him, you need to spend all day with him to learn about your duties until he returns. We have some packing to do, too.

"The doctor will meet with Lise in Oslo, and Sonja will send some of your outgrown clothes with him. Your sister can barter for sizes that fit you better. None of your mama's or mine or Lise's can be altered to fit your long waist and wide shoulders."

Just as she was feeling the buoyancy of a new challenge, Mari felt a twinge of resentment. "Why couldn't I look like the women in our family instead of the men?"

Bestemor pushed away from the table and stood up. She took her granddaughter's hands and pulled her to her feet. With one hand tilting Mari's chin, she scrutinized her from head to toe.

Mari didn't realize she had spoken her thoughts aloud. She felt her face flush and shuffled toward her chair.

"Nei, you stay right there, young lady!" Bestemor circled her slowly, tipping her head from side to side, squinting one eye and then the other, like an artist examining a bowl of fruit to be painted. She pointed to the framed prayer of grace that hung on the far kitchen wall. "Now read that to me, from here."

"Bestemor, you know what that says. We say the blessing at every meal." Mari couldn't suppress a grin at her grandma's silly antics.

"Can you *SEE* the words from here? Are they clear or blurry?"

"They are perfectly clear. Why?"

"Because, my no-longer-little-one, if your vision isn't the problem, you need to look in a mirror more often." She twirled her finger, directing Mari to turn around.

When they were face to face again, she continued. "You have wonderful features from your Papa, yes, but you do *not* look like a man! Sonja and I agree you are growing into a beautiful young lady. Here you spend all your time with two older women who are always busy and tired. Young people should be with young people, then you'd see through their eyes what a pretty girl you are."

Mari felt the blood rush to her face again. Was there truth in Bestemor's words? She had been so relieved to be "only" thirteen on her next birthday that she'd lost sight of the fact she would be a teenager in a few weeks.

Mari spent the rest of the day with the doctor. He was convinced that Mari could do what was needed, which was mostly delivering some prescriptions and tonics that were all prepared and carefully labeled with detailed instructions. He explained which patients needed help with routine treatments, and who to call on if something serious developed.

Before sunset that afternoon Mari made her way up to the picnic glade for a visit with Odin. Crusty snow covered his marker, but she knew exactly where to find him. She spent several minutes telling him her plans and explaining why she might not visit as often in the coming weeks. She lingered as long as possible, returning to home just minutes before curfew.

Inside the cottage door a suitcase stood ready along with a basket holding two jars of jams for Lise: currant and blueberry. Papa would take them to Doctor Olsen before departure time for the night train.

They shared a quiet meal of hearty soup and stoneloaf. After dinner, Mama set a saucer with custard on the table and handed each of them a spoon. "Compliments of the house," she joked. Whenever morsels of rare treats made their way from the main house to the cottage, this was her explanation.

Papa took a spoonful of custard and held it up as if to offer a toast. The others did the same. He began to speak but stopped, cleared his throat, then remained silent for several minutes. He swallowed hard, cleared his throat again, and finally words came. His voice was thick, a bit scratchy.

"To a safe journey for Doctor Olsen, and to safety for us all in the days to come. No matter what happens to any of us, we are always together in our hearts. God bless Norway."

"Amen," Mama and Bestemor said.

Mari thought of Bjorn and Erik, of the letter signed by Mama and Papa. She struggled to moisten her suddenly dry mouth.

"Amen," she murmured, and lifted her spoon to her lips.

Chapter Twenty-Six

Cracking Down

February 10.

Wonderful news, Bjorn!

Mama and Papa are safe! All the parents are. Everyone did exactly as Papa said they would and stood together against Quisling's orders. Two who were suspected of organizing the action to resist spent a night in jail, but nothing was proved and no one else was even questioned about it.

Papa says the same is true for the train worker unions, engineers, and even the clergy and physician groups. And so far Quisling has stayed silent, as if his orders were never issued. I'm so relieved!

Papa warned that a response could come later, though, so we must be on guard. Leif insisted that bigger trouble is still coming, bigger than we can imagine. But I think that's just more of his bluster. I hope I am right about that.

February 13.

Did you hear the terrible news, Bjorn? More than a thousand teachers all across Norway were arrested for refusing to join the NS union and sign agreements that would dictate what they teach.

It's just a few teachers from each school, of course. It's meant to scare the others into signing Quisling's contracts. The worst part is that MR. JENSEN was the teacher arrested from Ytre Arna, along with two other teachers from Indre Arna and Garnes. We heard nothing but rumors about where they were taken or what is happening to them.

I wish there was a way to know where they are, if they're safe. Papa says people are working to find out.

February 21.

Bjorn, I'm sorry I've missed so many days writing to you. Since I last wrote I've been busier than a Christmas nisse during Jul week. Thank goodness none of the doctor's patients had a crisis while he was away in Oslo, but little Johan needed to be checked several times a day. I've been helping the doctor care for him ever since. His cough shakes him to the core, but his mama is wonderful at calming him. Using warm camphor-soaked compresses on his chest and soothing him with steam vapors are the only medicines we can provide.

When I checked him today I was relieved that his temperature was normal, and his cough had improved. Maybe his crisis is over.

We have few modern medications to fight infection, mostly folk remedies, herbs and alcohol-based tonics.

Now that Doctor Olsen returned he wants me to keep working with the Molstads and several other families that need frequent visits. It frees him to deal with more serious needs. Poor nutrition and limited medicines cause many to suffer complications from easily treated conditions.

You are always in our prayers, Bjorn. Stay safe and warm. And healthy, too.

After Doctor Olsen caught up on his patients he delivered a clothing-stuffed suitcase to the cottage. During his trip to Oslo, Lise had outdone herself in exchanging Mari's outgrown clothing for new things. While the doctor warmed up with hot soup, Mari dug through the dresses and shirts, holding them up to her chin or waist one at a time, while Mama and Bestemor watched.

Doctor Olsen commented, "Those must be for you, Sonja, not Mari. They aren't the kinds of things a young girl wears."

He chuckled at the puzzled stares from three generations of female faces. "These are clothes for a grown woman. I'm an old bachelor, but I'm not blind!"

Bestemor patted his cheek and replied, "Since when are you paying attention to what anyone is wearing? Fever and rashes are the only details you notice about a person's appearance. If I dyed my hair purple, you'd start thinking about bruises!"

He shrugged, admitting Bestemor was probably right, and it took several minutes for the laughter in the room to subside.

Bestemor examined the collar on a particular dress. "These clothes are easily altered to fit Mari for now, and can be let out as she grows. Have you looked at our little one lately?"

Mari clutched a full-skirted dress at her waist and improvised a little dance. These would be the first new clothes she'd have in several years. "When Mama and Bestemor finish working on these, I'll be the best-dressed girl in town."

Her mother added, "Doctor, I think Mari will need some time off to help us sew. She knows the basics, but it's time she learns to stitch a seam and take a tuck. Of course, this will help her when she needs to sew up cuts and scrapes."

The doctor nodded. "Certainly. But it will be hard to make do without her. She's already a valuable assistant."

Mari was proud to hear that, but embarrassed at such praise. She steered the conversation in a new direction.

"Did Lise send the right medicines, Doctor?"

As soon as the words were out, Mari clamped a hand across her mouth. "I'm sorry. You told me not to mention that."

Her mother and grandma looked concerned and confused.

Mari didn't say another word.

After his return from Oslo, the doctor had shown her a smaller package from Lise. It was a book with a leather cover and a strap closure that snapped securely. He had opened the book carefully, then turned back the top twenty or so pages to reveal the truth: the center portion of the pages had been sliced out, creating a cavity packed with tightly wrapped and sealed envelopes.

Mari wanted to know more about the contents but hesitated to ask.

Doctor Olsen looked into Mari's worried eyes. "Don't feel bad about asking questions, Mari. One of the greatest crimes these invaders commit is making everyone, especially our youngest and brightest, resist our natural instincts to wonder and question the world."

He patted her hand and smiled, deepening the wrinkles on his weathered face. "Besides, what Lise gave me will be a part of your future."

"My future?"

She recalled the way he had provided black-market medicines to treat Bestemor's infected leg and Odin's injuries last year. She shuddered at the memory of Odin's stitches and swollen muzzle, grateful that in the past few months, she'd rarely caught a glimpse of the two soldiers, known locally as The Rat and Scarecrow, who had been involved in that injury a year ago last February.

Doctor Olsen continued, "I hate to say it, but medicine can do more than heal. Lise's trick to make Erik sick to avoid supporting Nazi projects is just one example. But it takes skill not to overdose or let the Germans catch on. The package from Lise will last me until my next visit to Bergen, where I have another source."

Mari's eyes widened as he spoke

"No, you're not ready to become involved in helping me administer these drugs. You have a talent for healing and comforting, not for making people ill. But you are a good observer. You can help me by reporting the exact nature of rashes, vomiting, and fevers, so I can know better how to adjust the doses. Together, we'll confront Germans where they are most vulnerable—their fear of germs!"

March 6.

I know, I know, I've been neglecting you, Bjorn. I can hear your voice in my ear every time I pass the pantry and hurry on to Doctor Olsen's without stopping to write to you. I don't know where to begin, though, with all that I've been doing and learning. And I've had to spend hours and hours at night keeping my studies up to date, and then reviewing all that the doctor is teaching me during the day.

When he returned from Oslo he had another proposal for me, one he discussed with Lise while they were together.

He asked if I could help him study how certain medicines should be used to heal and others to have, well, I'll just say other effects. He asked if I want to make the effort and take the risks.

That was one of the easiest questions I've answered since the occupation began. Of course!

Now I barely have a moment to worry about anything except my studies and my patients. They are at least under my control, not like dealing with the soldiers and Unghird. There's talk that schools will reopen in a week or two, and I really don't want to return. At least I've studied enough I don't think I've fallen behind.

I'll write more when I can, Bjorn, but it may not be soon. Stay strong and well.

March 31, 1942.

Astrid, Per and I celebrated Thor's birthday with mine. Mama saved some soup bones for him, but he'll have to use his imagination to get any flavor from them. They've already simmered in a soup pot for days.

At one year old, he's as smart and strong as anything—except Odin, of course. Odin would be five years old now, and I'll never stop missing him. The harsh winter is finally losing its grip, so I visit his grave most days.

Mama, Papa, and Bestemor tried to make my birthday special, working with the little we have. I should feel different, I suppose, but I don't. I wonder what becoming a teenager feels like when there's not a war going on?

The news that arrived today was the best possible gift—keeping up my school studies paid off! Everyone had to take the end-of-year tests when school resumed to determine our standing. Word came today that my scores were near perfect in every subject, even German language and history. My classes are over for the rest of the year!

Instead I'll work with Doctor Olsen as a clinic assistant. No more hiding from Leif at school, or avoiding Mr. Jensen's classroom. I can't stand seeing his Nazi replacement sitting at his desk.

If I do well in medical studies, the doctor will sponsor my independent work next year, too. I hope I never have to go to school again, at least until the Germans leave. School has turned into something you'd never recognize. It's like a prison. The teachers guard every word they say. And we do the same.

Soldiers teach youth fitness, language, and history classes, and then roam the halls or sit in other sessions. We know that they're watching and listening for any excuse to arrest someone.

Mr. Jensen was the only teacher taken from Ytre Arna. Of the thousand teachers they arrested, about half were released a few days later. Not him. I wonder if Leif reported all the negative things Mr. Jensen taught us about Hitler when we were in Lower School? Could that explain why he wasn't released?

After all the parents joined together and refused to let their children join Unghird, or NSUF, the bullying let up a bit, at least at school. I stay on guard, though, as I travel on my rounds for Doctor Olsen's patients. If a gang finds someone alone, they cause trouble. They run in packs, like rats, then brag about how brave they are.

I try to mask my true feelings about Hitler and NS from Leif, but I'm still not good at acting. He may have told his group to keep an eye on me.

Just how brave will they be when they're old enough to join the army? Leif still says he is eager to go. Hitler sends more and more German troops to live here, then recruits OUR boys and men to fight for him in Russia. Stalin's army is chewing up and spitting out the German troops, but both sides are ruthless. Jossing papers call Russia the "slaughterhouse front."

Chapter Twenty-Seven

Further Developments

Spring and Summer, 1942

April 4.

New arrivals swarm like an army of termites, destroying our country bite by bite. Poor Mr. Jensen's mother can't manage on her own since he was arrested. After the accident that killed her husband and damaged her hip and leg, she's always depended on her son to care for her.

Since she's too young for the elders' home, she joined Mrs. Nilsson's "family." At Mrs. Nilsson's she'll have help and company. Pooling their rations makes food go further, too.

When I think of soldiers living in Mr. Jensen's house while he's in a prison camp I want to scream!

Mrs. Jensen needs to use her wheelchair on

bad days, although sometimes she manages with a cane. Mr. Molstad and Doctor Olsen helped her move, especially getting up the steep front steps. I helped them rearrange beds and furniture so she can move about more easily. The kitchen door opens right onto the backyard garden so she can enjoy good weather days.

What a household they have now! Astrid is only fourteen, her mother is still young, and I think Mrs. Jensen is about Mama's age, although she seems older. Mrs. Nilsson says it takes three women to fill the space her two sons left vacant.

Add to that a cat who thinks he's a forest king, and Thor, a young dog who believes he's a Norse god!

There's been no word of Mrs. Nilsson's sons since they escaped to England with their fishing boat. Papa says they're probably shuttling refugees, agents, radios and weapons. No wonder she worries about them.

Mrs. Jensen is desperate for news of her son. She hasn't heard from him since they arrested all those teachers. And he must worry about her, too.

She wrote a letter to tell him where she's living now, but there's no address for the detention camp. Gestapo officers strut about in their black coats with Nazi Eagle insignias, acting like they run the world. Then they claim they don't know where to find their own prisoners. They took her letter but I doubt it will reach him.

April 9.

Classes were cancelled for an official celebration of the two-year anniversary of the invasion. Even though I have no classes I was required to attend. It was dreadful. We sang Nazi songs, watched Unghird parades, and heard speeches full of lies about Germany.

The Unghird "maintained order," and harassed people as we left for home. Leif's buddy Edvar stopped me and searched my bag. He was so rough with it I thought my clinic supplies would be damaged. When I snatched it back, he twisted my arm and pushed me against the wall, shouting threats in my face.

He's so strong that I couldn't get loose until Leif made a big show of "rescuing" me, which I admit I appreciated. Just when I was feeling grateful, he bragged to Edvar that he'd "make me pay" and "show proper respect." He wrapped his arm around me, whispered to play along, and kissed my cheek!

I had to leave with him to get away from Edvar. Leif linked his arm through mine and walked me all the way home. He insisted I'd be safer if they think he's my boyfriend, and he apologized for what he said to Edvar. What am I supposed to believe?

Boyfriend? He's not any kind of friend! This is the first time I've seen him in months, and I never know what he'll do. Maybe he's just trying to impress them. I don't know what to think. Two years ago none of this mattered.

May 17. Syttende Mai.

Today came and went as a regular Sunday. We toasted Lise and Erik's first anniversary with a sip of Bestemor's homemade akevitt. Uff da! Whatever she uses to "improvise" on the regular ingredients is no improvement!

Posters threatened imprisonment for anyone celebrating our Constitution Day. Extra patrols roamed the streets, especially Unghird. It was nothing like Lise's wedding day a year ago. I'll never forget the music and joy of that day.

The Jossing papers lifted our spirits with a special edition. There was a message from King Haakon VII, lots of cartoons and jokes about Quisling, and suggestions for hiding flags inside coat linings and shoes. Last night even more propaganda posters were destroyed and walls were painted with our real flags. Unghird members had to spend most of the next day whitewashing over them and putting up more NS propaganda.

They weren't happy about that, but I enjoyed watching them!

May 31.

Per returned from a week in Bergen where he saw a Jewish detention camp not far from the city. He didn't know Mr. Meier well, but he thinks he might have seen him in a labor squad working outside of the camp. Prisoners break up boulders and load chunks on trucks for transport to bunkers. Papa says the bunkers are covering the coast faster than rock moss.

Per said the Jewish prisoners looked like skeletons. They do the hardest work using simple hand tools.

He was looking for Mr. Jensen, but a local man told him that the teachers are in a separate camp in the far north. Rumors say they do the same kind of back-breaking work. They can come home if they sign papers promising to teach German lies, but few have agreed. I'm not surprised.

I didn't tell Mrs. Jensen about this, even though I see her often.

Mrs. Jensen's move was good for everyone, it seems, even if it's a crowded life. Mrs. Nilsson is her sassy self in safe company. She seems to worry less about her sons now, but Bestemor says she's just getting better at hiding her fears.

June 12.

What a sweltering day, but I'm not complaining even when summer sun burns through my clothes and toasts me to the bone. Winter is finally behind us. I hope next winter is milder—food and fuel shortages made it nearly impossible to stay warm and fed. Snow at the picnic glade just disappeared a few weeks ago, even the last bits in the north slope shadows.

I visit Odin several times each week, but I think of him every day.

Working with Doctor Olsen takes most of my time. I worry I'll make mistakes, so I study for hours each night learning about medicines and treatments. The health of the elders is being stretched to the limits, and what I can provide isn't enough.

You'd be so proud of Bestemor, though. She must be made of iron—she seems stronger than ever.

Bjorn, you said I was ready to handle this, but what if you were wrong? What if I make mistakes that harm someone?

June 17.

Since mid-April, the trapping, fishing and gardening have been outstanding. Now that their classes have ended, Per and Astrid join me sometimes. I've missed them, and Thor, too. When we're able to meet and catch up on news, it's almost like old times.

Per shares government news, including more laws against Jews. It's ridiculous, and so hateful. Papa says Hitler's man in Oslo, Terboven, has lost patience with Quisling. He plans to take over and drop an "iron fist" on Jews. What more can he do to make life harder for them than it is now?

When I asked, Papa just shrugged. He looked so sad. I'm sure he's sparing me the truth.

Chapter Twenty-Eight

Confusion in the Garden

July, 1942

"Stubborn weeds. Stop fighting!"

Mari dropped her hoe and wiped a corner of her apron across her sweaty face. She'd been working in the village garden for more than an hour. The intense sun was directly overhead, and she was already late to meet the doctor.

Before rationing she'd have walked away from this last stubborn bit. Now it was crucial to pick off every potato bug, squish every cabbageworm, and clear every weed. Supplies in the stores were meager, poor quality, and expensive. Even when she shopped with enough ration cards, she might wait in long lines only to reach the counter and find the shelves were bare.

Mari gripped the hoe and directed her frustration at the weeds. She was not about to sacrifice a meal without a fight. Thistles had sprouted in the shadowy spaces under curling cucumber vines, hidden until their roots were anchored deep in the soil. She'd managed to remove all but this one last thistle. With a furious hack she took off the top of the remaining intruder, but severed a cucumber vine in the process. The fallen squash stem had a half dozen swelling yellow buds—food that would never develop.

"Arghhh!" She dropped to her knees and seized the stub of the thistle stem with both hands, yanking with all her might. The prickly spines dug into her fingers but she refused to surrender.

"I. Will. Get. You. Out!"

With each word she gripped harder, twisting slightly, and felt the roots shift. On her last word they released, and she plopped backward to land in the dirt.

Laughter startled her. An Unghird pack was standing just outside the garden fence. Mari's face was already so red from heat and exertion it may not have shown, but she felt a sudden deep blush of embarrassment and anger.

Mari recognized most of them from school, but none she knew well. Then, at the outskirts of the pack, she saw Leif. She glared at them all, but especially at him. A little loyalty didn't seem too much to expect.

Her temper boiled when the boys pointed at her and laughed harder before heading off to make trouble for someone else. But Leif stayed behind and swung open the gate to join her inside the community garden.

"What do you want? Did you come to insult me in person?" Mari looked up but stayed on the ground.

The thistle nettles were stinging now, and her gaze dropped from Leif to her palms. Amid the garden grime on her hands she spied dozens of spiny needles embedded in her skin, like a fistful of splinters. She stifled a moan of pain. She refused to let Leif hear her suffer.

He crouched beside her and took her hands in his to examine them.

"No, Mari. I just thought you might need my help." He nodded toward her open palms. His gentle tone surprised her.

Then he pulled a scouting knife from his pocket and flipped out a short narrow blade. Instinctively she clenched her hands and pulled them into her lap, making them sting even more.

"It's okay, Mari, I can help. You just have to trust me." He covered her right hand, tugged gently, and rested it in his own palm. "Please. I won't hurt you."

The knife blade was small and clean; his hands were steady. He looked and sounded like the friend she'd always known.

She uncurled her fingers and held her breath.

Leif's head dipped closer to her palm and he examined each penetrating nettle. One by one he gripped an exposed spine between his thumb and the tip of the small blade, worked it gently, and slid it out from under her skin. After five or six successes she was able to breathe, grateful for his help. Soon he was working on her left hand. Before long it, too, was cleared of the painful spines.

"That does it." He smiled a familiar smile. "I'd say I told you so, but you've been stung enough for one day."

His smug smile returned, but wasn't quite so annoying now that the burning pain was relieved.

"Where did you learn to do that? Bestemor uses a needle and has to dig a bit to get out thorns and slivers. This was much easier. I could use your technique in the clinic."

"My uncle gave me this knife, and he taught me. It doesn't work when they're buried under the skin, only when the troublemakers remain a bit above the surface."

He folded the blade back into his knife. "You might want to clean up now." He gestured toward the faucet at the edge of the garden, then stood and offered his hand.

"Tusen takk, Leif." She accepted his help, then hurried to the faucet where she scrubbed her hands vigorously.

Leif followed her, soaked a clean handkerchief, and wrung it out. She reached for it but he pulled back and said, "First things first." He cupped her chin with one hand and began wiping her forehead and nose.

She was so startled it took a moment to react, then she pulled back and demanded, "What are you doing?"

He chuckled and handed her the cloth. "You do it, then." He pointed toward her dirty apron and added, "Next time you wipe your face, use something clean."

She looked at the formerly white handkerchief and saw that it was smeared with garden soil he'd wiped from her face. She laughed while rinsing it again, then wiped her face thoroughly. She handed him his cloth and looked away.

"That's better," he said. "How are your hands feeling?"

She examined her palms and was pleased to see how much the cold water had helped. "I'll ask Mrs. Nilsson what to use on them when I drop off her vegetables. She has an herbal treatment for everything."

Leif offered to help with deliveries. Mari was already running late, so she accepted even though his company and conversation weren't really welcome.

As they walked Leif said, "I expected to see you around town more often this summer with Astrid, Per, and Thor. Thor's turned into a terrific dog. When Per gave him to you as a puppy at our graduation I was surprised, but even more curious. Why did you want Astrid to take him? Any regrets about that?"

Before speaking Mari glanced in both directions. The Unghird boys were gathered a few blocks down the street, and there were no soldiers in sight. She chose her words carefully and dropped her voice. "Not really. I enjoy helping Astrid with Thor, but until the Germans are gone I won't have another dog. Not after Odin."

Leif nodded slightly, scanning the streets as well. "The Germans are here to stay, Mari. There's no point in waiting, you should just get another dog now."

She struggled to stay silent, but simmering anger made her words come out clipped and intense. "After what they did to Odin? Never! I won't take that chance with another dog of my own. And don't get too confident. Hitler's troops will be gone sooner than you think. I know it!"

"Well, if *you* were fighting them the way you fought those weeds, I'd believe it!" He laughed a bit, but something about it sounded strained.

Loud voices interrupted their debate. Leif said, "Wait here," and ran around the corner to investigate. In just a few moments he returned.

He waved farewell and jogged toward the corner. She wanted to ask why but hesitated, suspecting it had to do with his Unghird pals.

Before disappearing into the side street, he stopped suddenly and called, "Go straight home, Mari." He was out of sight in seconds.

Chapter Twenty-Nine

Secrets Within Secrets

August, 1942

By late summer Mari's confidence in treating simple injuries and illnesses grew. Most days she would get the laundry washed and hung outside, then hurry to the clinic in the doctor's parlor. She checked and treated patients with simple complaints on her own, and made others more comfortable until the doctor could see them.

One morning after things quieted down, she hurried home to fold laundry and start ironing. The soldiers hadn't yet returned from their patrol and the sheets weren't dry, so she returned to the cottage. Doctor Olsen had said she could come in later that day, so she thought she might have a chance to write a few words to Bjorn. Her days were passing in a blur, so she wrote less often. This was a chance to sort out highlights and catch him up.

She climbed the ladder, knelt on the carpet, and adjusted the hatch.

What was that? She froze, straining to locate a source for the noise she heard. Had she forgotten to lock the door?

Long minutes passed in silence.

She heard nothing from the main floor, but her panicked reaction to that initial sound lingered. Finally, her pulse slowed and she edged quietly toward the footstool that had her journal in it.

There it was again.

The sound came from the small attic alcove above the furnace room. In winter she sometimes felt vibrations through the floor when the furnace turned on, but this was summer.

Could it be a mouse, or some other creature? She stayed still, turning her head to catch even the slightest sound.

Nothing.

Her imagination was getting the best of her. If something had worked its way into that space she should investigate, but she wasn't going in there blind.

With as little noise as possible, she lowered herself back down through the hatch to get Papa's flashlight. It wasn't on the shelf near the front door, but she checked the lock while she was there. Eventually she found the flashlight on a shelf in the furnace room.

That's when she heard it—that scraping sound was directly overhead.

She climbed the ladder and raised the hatch. If she could see what it was she'd set a snare and save Papa any extra work.

When she reached the bookcase, the opening to the small alcove was blocked by a stack of framed posters.

A mouse hadn't done that.

Keeping her head down she moved as quietly as possible toward the hatch.

Before she'd taken even a few steps a hand covered her mouth and her arm twisted behind her. She was pulled backward, lowered to sit on the floor, and dragged next to the chimney. After a moment of shock, her free hand clawed at the hand covering her mouth.

The grip on her wrist eased a bit, and she struggled harder.

"Don't scream, please. I won't hurt you."

It was a man's voice, speaking English. Mr. Jensen had taught them English during the last two years of Lower School, and portions of BBC reports were in English, although most were in Norwegian.

She craned her head to one side then the other but she couldn't see her attacker clearly.

"Please. Don't scream. I won't hurt you. I thought you were one of the Krauts."

Her arm was released and the man knelt at her side, his hand still covering her mouth.

He was about Bjorn's age, dressed in a uniform she'd never seen before. His dark eyes pleaded with her. One sleeve was ripped at the shoulder, and he had a bloody bandage on his forehead.

"Will you stay quiet? Please?"

She nodded, doubting she could force her way past the injured man to reach the hatch. He moved his hand from her mouth to her shoulder, pressing her against the chimney.

She worked at finding the right words in English. "Who are you? Why are you here?" she whispered.

"First, who are *you?* What are YOU doing here?" He was suddenly more soldier-like, like an officer grilling a new recruit.

Maybe he was from a special branch of the Gestapo, trying to trap her.

Mari was confused, but thought it best to answer. "I live here." She wondered if he had found her notebook.

"You live here? Anders said his daughter sometimes comes up here to read or write, but not often. He said he'd teach her our signal. Is that who you are?"

She struggled to understand what he was saying. "What is . . . 'our signal'? Who *are* you?"

It was the stranger's turn to look flustered and confused. Mari's limited medical experience told her the man was probably in pain and needed help. She chose her limited English words carefully.

"You are hurt. I work with doctor." She slowly reached out to feel his forehead, which was hot. She lifted the edge of his bandage to find a nasty gash, inflamed and seeping.

"Wait here."

Surprisingly, he made no effort to stop her. She hurried down to the bathroom and soaked two clean washcloths with warm soapy water.

She returned and spent several minutes cleaning and examining the gash. It needed stitches, but not until the infection cleared. She used a small towel to rewrap his wound. Next she probed through the torn shirt and uniform to find that his shoulder was bruised, scraped, and swollen, but not broken.

He winced now and then as she poked and prodded, but he endured until she finished. Then he flashed a smile. "For such a young lass, you're a right good nurse. I apologize for scaring the stuffing out of you before. I've been jumpy as a flea on a field hound, knowing there's a pack of wolves prowling just beyond those walls. When I heard someone come up without the signal, I was sure you were one of 'em."

She wasn't clear on everything he had said in English, but Mari needed answers.

"Who is Anders? Why are you here?"

"Well, missy, you make as good an interrogator as you do a medic, don'cha now?" He smiled again. "If you are who you say you are, you already know that Anders is your father. He offered me the use of this lovely little apartment for my brief stay in your beautiful country."

He gestured toward the dark, cramped alcove. His words and accent were foreign, but his face had the same look as Bjorn's and Per's when teasing.

She crawled over to the hatch, leaned down to listen, and returned. Again she chose her words carefully, hoping they made sense. "If my father brings you here, you stay here. Have you had food today? I will bring you some, now. Soldiers come back soon."

"I could do with some fish and chips, but I doubt they're on the menu. I'll be fine, lass, you'd best be out of here now. Much obliged for your help." He waved her away and pointed to the hatch.

"Wait here." She dropped through the hatch, collected two jars of canned beans, a jar of plums, two large towels, and a blanket. In very little time she arranged a makeshift mat on the floor inside the alcove with a rolled-towel pillow. The soldier seemed as tall as Papa, but he'd be able to get some sleep if he stretched his legs into the lowest area near the wall. From the looks of him, he needed sleep as much as he did medical treatment.

Mari spoke slowly and hoped he would understand her. "Safer to stay in here. Eat and rest. Someone come back when more safe. Please, not hurt me when I come?" She smiled and hoped she had said in English what she intended.

"You've made a right cozy campsite for me, miss. When your papa comes, he does this. . . ." He tapped a pattern on the floor. "Then I know not to tackle an intruder with my massive brute force. Give it a try."

She tapped, but he corrected her. Then she did it right.

"There, you see, if you give me that little signal you'll be welcome anytime you want to visit."

She smiled at his relentless good humor in defiance of his weak condition and dangerous situation.

She stacked the framed posters back over the opening to the alcove. "Rest. Stay quiet."

Mari's day dragged on endlessly, despite being busier than usual. She visited her list of patients in their homes, prepared supplies for the next day, and returned home to study.

All the while her mind was working on the puzzle of the stranger's identity. Papa wouldn't come home until late, and she couldn't say a word to anyone else.

The German patrol returned in late afternoon, and the garden was filled with their smoke and chatter, leaving her feeling trapped in the cottage and helpless. It wasn't hard to imagine how the man in the attic must feel, knowing he could hear them, too.

When Papa finally arrived, he had no sooner clicked the lock shut than Mari dragged him to the back of the kitchen.

"Papa, did you hide someone in the attic?"

What if he said no?

His eyes got big, and his answer was so long in coming she wondered if the man overhead had lied to her.

"Little one, tell me what you know." He gripped her elbows and leaned in close.

Now she was as irritated as she was afraid. "Did you hide someone up there or not? Because someone *is* there, right this minute, and he's hurt! Why didn't you tell me?"

Her father covered his face with his hands, then ran his fingers through his hair. "Achh, you should never have been involved in this."

"In what? Tell me, because I *am* involved, and his wound needs treatment. But for now sleep is more important. Why is he here? How long will he stay?"

While the soup simmered on the stove, Papa tried to explain. The man was an English agent who was injured in a fall in the rugged hills of the Norwegian interior. He had been trying to reach a resistance unit. The men he was trying to contact had found him just in time, before the weather, or wild animals, or German patrols did him in.

Papa said the Brits should have sent mountain-trained agents. But that advice was too late for this one. He had been brought secretly back to the shores of Sørfjord to wait for a boat to take him back to England.

Papa had agreed to hide him but had only hours to decide the best place to do that. The attic made more sense than the garage, as it would be easier to check on him and take him food. The man would leave as soon as conditions were right. If the weather held, that would happen two nights from now.

Papa had met him and two men from the resistance unit out on a mountain trails very early that morning, slipping the wounded man into the house and helping him up into the attic and into the alcove while the rest of the family was sound asleep.

"I thought you would be off to the clinic after doing the laundry today, Mari, as usual. I was going to tell all of you about our visitor at supper tonight."

Papa shared few other details, but Mari sensed that the little fishing skiff tied at their pier was involved. She was to have no part in that operation.

But she could help the man recover enough to travel safely.

She pictured Bjorn in such a situation.

"Papa, I want to help."

Papa wasn't sure at first that her involvement was a good idea, but Mari would not accept no for an answer. Finally, he relented. He made sure she had the signal correct, and Mari made a list of needed medical supplies. Since the Brit was fed and resting, they decided not to wake him until morning.

Chapter Thirty

Time To Choose

His name, she had learned, was Bernie. On the night the English soldier left, just a few days after Mari first met him, his wound was dry and his fever had eased. Her role in that healing was simple, she realized, compared to the risks others took to orchestrate his rescue: a series of resistance workers rowed him, covered, at the bottom of little skiffs, transferred from one village to the next, until they arranged to meet a fishing vessel, manned by Norwegian sailors, the so-called Shetland Bus route.

In a week's time Mari had removed all signs of their visitor from the alcove, but his presence lingered, like a friendly ghost, in the attic.

She admired his constant smile despite facing pain and unimaginable dangers. She had even begun to understand his funny English expressions and accent. She especially appreciated "jumpy as a flea on a field hound." That described exactly how she felt most of the last two years.

After Bernie was gone, Mari pestered Papa for any news about him. She worried about him and was desperate to know if he had reached England. Her questions finally stopped when Papa told her they weren't likely to *ever* learn his fate.

What they *did* learn in September was that Hitler's man in Oslo, Terboven, was back in charge of their country. Terboven allowed Quisling to keep his title, but his authority was in name only. The hundreds of laws Quisling had imposed had seen little effect and were mostly ignored. The teachers in labor camps still refused to cooperate, no matter what hardships they were forced to endure.

Terboven's Gestapo leadership took a different approach. They ramped up their demands, but this time using steel boots and iron fists. In particular, Terboven was determined to rid Norway of "Jewish vermin." From the earliest days of occupation the ration allowances for Jews had been half the amount for other citizens. Now rations for Jews were halved again. Camps were filling up, with an eventual goal to arrest every Jewish person on record, starting with the men.

One evening after dinner Papa lit his pipe, then put it down and cleared his throat. "We have a decision to make. If we proceed, *every one* of us must agree."

After-dinner discussions were generally serious, but this sounded different. His tone gripped Mari's attention. She looked at Mama and Bestemor, who also sat up at Papa's statement.

He continued. "It won't be as simple as helping the Brit. But we have a chance to help several Jewish citizens escape to England."

Three heads leaned in closer, straining to catch every word.

"There are rumors that the Nazis plan to round up every last Jewish person. And we've heard they want to send all Jews to special work camps closer to Germany. Some Jews are convinced the war will end soon and nothing terrible will happen, but others still living in eastern Norway, mostly from Olso, want to escape across the border to safety in Sweden."

Mari pictured her friend Sarah's family. They had left Ytre Arna, tucked against the mountains on the west coast, to journey north. They likely slipped across the Swedish border somewhere along the thousand miles of dense forests that stretched along the far eastern edge of Norway. At least Mari hoped they had escaped in those early days of occupation.

"How can we help more from here escape all the way to Sweden, Papa?"

"We can't. Germans stalk the countryside like cats on the prowl, and their patrols increase week by week. Anyone trying to make that trip to Sweden now, especially from here in the west, would surely be captured."

She scoured his face for hints about what would come next.

"Where we live gives us a different option. Boats like

the one that saved the Brit bring messages and equipment from England. Sometimes they have space to take a few lucky passengers back with them."

Is that what he was asking? Would they take the risk of hiding someone here and helping them escape like Bernie?

How could they not?

Before Papa accepted their unanimous agreement, he described the situation fully. This would be for a longer stay, and it would be a family. A Jewish woman had been on the run with her two children since her husband was arrested in August. They survived by hiking and hiding in the woods for several weeks, slowly making their way to the coast. Now they were half-starved and exhausted. Arranging for their escape would take time, every minute of which would put them all at great risk.

"Understand this," Papa warned. "Punishment for hiding Bernie would have been severe, but if this Jewish family is discovered here, we could face execution." He took a moment and held the gaze of each of them, ending with Mari.

"All of us. Believe me, baby girl, I never thought I would ask such a thing of you. If you hadn't already shown your bravery helping the agent, I would pass this on to someone else. Our location is the ideal one to hide them for a longer time and also to make the fjord connections necessary for their escape. The others I've talked with agree that bringing them here, under the very noses of the German soldiers, might be the last place anyone would suspect such a family to be hiding."

Mari nodded as she saw the heartbreak in his eyes, and she reached across the table to squeeze his hand.

"I know, Papa, we can do this."

Within a week a family was living in the attic.

Mari had lined the alcove floor with old rugs and blankets. All three—one adult and two children—would sleep in there and stay hidden, unless someone in Mari's family signaled them to come out. It was cramped, but the padding meant they could shift around a bit without making noise. For short periods during the day, when they were allowed to come out to the slightly larger, sunlit space in the main part of the attic, the children could play quietly. Mari allowed them to play with the toy collection from Bjorn's childhood that Lise discovered during her visit. Mari was certain that he would approve.

After weeks starving and hiding on the mountainside, the three refugees were relieved to arrive at the house. Although they had to stay in the attic, and mostly in the tiny alcove, at least it was warm and dry, and they were fed.

Everyone used first names only. Their original home was Hardanger province, where Rachel's husband had been arrested. The two little daughters, Eva and Gilda, were as sweet as June berries. Even when they lived at home in Hardanger, before the arrest, they were barely surviving on half-rations. After the arrest, Rachel told her neighbors she and the girls were going north to work on a farm. Instead they'd been running and hiding ever since, eating from the wild and from trash, which contained few edibles.

Mari wondered how they had survived for so long, even in summer. It was no surprise that Rachel was ill, and all three, especially the children, were little more than skin and bones.

When the soldiers were away from the house and her chores were completed, Mari tended to the family's needs. She brought them food, provided medical care, and shared news. They couldn't risk going down to use the bathroom, but Mari shuttled water, soap, and towels to them. She also collected and disposed of their waste. Of course it was embarrassing at first, but they all adjusted quickly.

If she had time, Mari took up a favorite children's book and read quietly to Eva and Gilda, who sat as still as churchmice, eyes wide, soaking in every word.

Cottage meals for Mari's family became broth and vegetable scraps. Most of their family food was used to fortify the guests for their coming trip across the North Sea. Papa had no guarantees, however, about how long it would be until a boat could be arranged for their escape.

Rachel's congestion was serious, and slow to improve. Mari wanted to use towel compresses soaked with hot oil and camphor on Rachel's chest, as she did with so many others. But the pungent odors that treatment created could cause suspicion if soldiers entered the cottage.

Goatman's unexpected appearances still plagued Mari. She had found him in the cellar of the main house one morning when she arrived. He was rummaging through the family's food shelves and made no secret of taking a jar of plum jelly before leaving. Another day he insisted on carrying her laundry basket into the cottage for her, although he waited for her to unlock the door that time. They had never again found the cottage door unlocked, but that proved nothing.

Had he heard or seen something from the attic window and come to investigate? She managed to usher him back out, but she later warned Rachel and the girls to be extra quiet. What if Goatman returned again? He seemed to have a thing about snooping about the place.

As for Eva's and Gilda's health, Mari had little to offer. The girls' teeth and gums were in bad shape from poor diet and hygiene. Mari had no way to get milk for them. If only a troll would turn Goatman into a nanny goat, she'd tie it in the garden and bring fresh milk to the girls every day.

Without magic, though, the best she could do was show Rachel how to use gauze and iodine to gently rub their gums when the pain was intolerable. It tasted awful, but numbed their mouths a bit.

As the days passed, to Mari's relief, all three of the hidden family members began edging back toward health. Bit by bit, they were adding more flesh to their bones than when they arrived.

Chapter Thirty-One

Success and Sadness

Fall and Winter, 1942

The original plan was for Rachel's family to leave in September during the darkness of the new moon. Just a few days before that, Papa learned that someone in the area was suspicious. German patrols on land and on the fjord increased, especially along the waterfront. Their guests would have to stay in the attic until October's new moon when they would try again.

Mari was terrified about the North Sea passage the family would make and wished Rachel's family could stay with them until the war ended. There was no denying, though, that the risks to both families increased each day they remained.

Battles in the North Sea and in the waters around the British Isles were the subject of many news broadcasts. One night BBC reported that a German U-boat had been sunk, then the next night they announced that a Norwegian ship had not returned from its run. Was it a fishing boat like the one Mrs. Nilsson's sons captained? Names of boats weren't given, so there was no way of knowing if a missing boat belonged to the Nilsson men or not.

Papa said that was the kind of boat Rachel and her girls would have been on, so the delay might have saved their lives. He called the loss tragic, but the daring fishing-boat trips provided the only hope for Jews and others to escape on the west coast. The BBC called this brave fleet the Shetland Bus, since the boats were based in Scotland's Shetland Islands. They made frequent trips across the stormy North Sea to supply the Norwegian resistance and evacuate all sorts of passengers to freedom.

Mrs. Nilsson knew how vital her sons' work was, but Mari saw the constant worry in her eyes, even when she spoke of other things. Was Mrs. Nilsson not as good at hiding it, or was Mari getting better at recognizing the pain lurking behind her cheerful banter?

While their guest family hid in the attic, Mari postponed writing her journal letters to Bjorn. She'd catch up when Rachel and the girls were gone. Since Bjorn would have to wait till the end of the war to read her letters, Mari knew it was fine to wait to write more.

It was odd, but Mari felt more certain than ever that Bjorn was alive and that he would return to them some day.

Her optimism increased greatly when their guests were able to leave during the October new moon. German patrols had dropped to normal, and Papa proceeded with the plan to escape by sea. Rachel's congestion had improved, so she could travel in the damp night air without triggering coughing spells that might give them away.

When it was finally time to leave, the girls clung to Mari and begged her to go with them. She struggled to hold back her tears and told little Eva and Gilda there was a surprise waiting in Rachel's pack, but not to peek until they reached Britain. She had squeezed two of their favorite books among their things. Inside each she had written, "I'll never forget you. Remember me. Love, Mari."

After their hidden visitors left, Mari's family ate better again with fewer mouths to share their food. There was little satisfaction in that, though, after seeing with their own eyes what was being done to the Jews. More than two years had passed since Mari had witnessed soldiers drag Mr. Meier down the mountain, injured and helpless. That scene terrified her and sometimes haunted her dreams.

The day she finally saw him again was equally unforgettable.

At least she thought the man she saw was Mr. Meier.

She was biking along the roadway after checking on Mrs. Magnussen's injured foot when a convoy passed by. Each truck seemed to have a soldier driving and a Gestapo officer in the cab, but the open beds were crammed with prisoners, packed like sardines. Their heads were shaved and their striped uniforms were ragged and filthy. Some had threadbare blankets around their shoulders, but most had no protection from the cold. As the trucks passed by, Mari could see each had two soldiers riding in back, rifles poised to prevent escapes.

The first truck rumbled past before she realized what she was seeing. When the next one approached she hopped off her bike and watched from a safe place off the road. The prisoners gazed out at the passing countryside, looking exhausted and weakened. Mari was flooded with pangs of sympathy and intense anger.

Why were Jews being treated so badly? They were Norwegians, too. They posed no more threat to the Germans than any other Norwegians did.

Then, to her shock, she was almost certain she saw Mr. Meier in the third truck. He was so shriveled and skeletal that she couldn't be sure. The truck disappeared around a bend before she could cry out or wave.

At least, if she was right, he was still alive.

When Mari told her family, Papa said that he had heard confirmation that the Nazis were preparing to transport every Norwegian Jew to Germany. Papa said that a ship was reported waiting in Oslo harbor to take them to special "work camps" in Germany.

Mari could hardly imagine why this was happening. Why were the Nazis so terrible to people who had done them no harm?

The Nazi iron fist was coming down hard on the

underground papers, too. Printing or circulating secret newspapers was ruled punishable by death. Those involved had to be even more careful than in the past, but no one planned to stop reading or sharing the Jossing papers.

Including Mari.

Greta told her the actual printing of the papers was being moved from place to place, sometimes every week. She still helped her father, writing some articles and editing others. The relentless Nazi propaganda and isolation made that risk necessary.

Resistance papers offered credible news, satirical cartoons, and mocking jokes to remind the people of their common cause. The Jossing papers urged people to bind together as loyal Norwegians. Because of the papers, some people who joined NS in the early months disavowed the Nazis and gave up their privileges.

Even so, Mari had to question if those families were actually trustworthy now, or if there was a chance they were still "striped" and reporting back to the Germans.

After what felt like an endless stream of autumn worry, Mari was excited to have some *good* news to share at dinner.

"Bestemor, for now you can't even let Mrs. Nilsson know about this. Not until he comes home." Mari knew that those two lifelong friends shared everything, but this was a special case.

Bestemor scolded, "We all know that the teachers

were released from the labor camps last week, Mari."

Papa speculated, "The released teachers might not make it home for a few months. Mr. Jensen could be moving from town to town along the way. If she tried to write to him, the letters would trail behind."

"Please," Mari begged, "just let me explain."

Mama refilled Mari's cup. "Yes, do, little one. How is it that you happen to know so much about Mr. Jensen's release?"

"I know so much because I saw him today—in Doctor Olsen's bedroom!"

She waited for their startled expressions and questions to subside. For once it was her turn to wear a smug smile.

"He arrived two days ago, in secret, but he wants no one else to know for now. He is in such a sorry state his recovery will be slow and difficult. He doesn't want to see his mother until he heals and gets some strength back. Doctor Olsen agreed, but only if he could at least let Mrs. Jensen know he had gotten word that her son was safe and would be home soon."

"He's here? In Ytre Arna?" Bestemor insisted that his mother should be allowed to see him, no matter his condition. "She's been out of her mind with worry for months now. Doctor Olsen doesn't understand how a mother feels about her child."

For once in her life Mari dared to scold her grandmother. "You didn't see him. I did, and I barely recognized him. He's afraid that seeing him in this condition would be more than she could bear."

Reluctantly, Bestemor nodded her understanding.

Mari shared a bit more. "He was as starved as the Jews on the trucks I told you about. He has open sores and bruises and is as weak as a baby. He says almost nothing about his time in the camp, except that in the early days, nine months ago, a few teachers gave in to Quisling's demands. After that the rest refused, no matter what was done to them. I asked why they were released now. He thinks the Germans just got tired of keeping them and gave up."

Papa nodded knowingly. "Quisling is out of power, but when the teachers were released last week, he announced that he 'taught the teachers a lesson.'"

Mama wondered, "Does Mr. Jensen know you've told us? Could *we* visit him?"

"Not yet, Mama. The doctor says we should let the man rest and heal, and have some control over his own life until he feels ready to return to the world. He allowed me to tell you all only if you made a promise of secrecy."

Bestemor wiped her eyes. "I'm sorry I argued. I'll do whatever the poor man wants. I'll make some special foods you can deliver to help him recover, and I promise to respect his wishes."

Papa took a long draw on his pipe. "Well, no matter what Quisling says, the Jossing papers got it right—this is another defeat for the Germans. But teachers like Mr. Jensen were casualties of the battle."

Chapter Thirty-Two

Thor is Threatened

Mari and her family hovered at the edges of the large crowd with the Nilsson household, the Molstads, and Doctor Olsen. They resented being forced to attend a celebration of the "purification" of their German "Fortress in the North." The Nazi mayor of Ytre Arna went on and on about the many evils Jews had caused for centuries.

Mari squeezed Bestemor's hand and stared at the ground. No amount of acting could mask her disgust at his words.

When he finally stopped speaking, a band played Hitler's favorite music. Unghird circulated to make sure everyone participated. Papa did his part, dancing with Mama. Mari guessed he was singing their special song in her ear. Bestemor and Mrs. Nilsson did a little waltz, and the doctor led Mrs. Tomasson in a lively polka. Little Johan adored Mari, and she swung him on her hip in circles.

Then Leif appeared and asked Mari to dance.

"Nei, takk, I have a partner." She circled so her back

was toward him.

Leif looked back at Unghird members and tugged her arm. "Just do as I say for once."

His scowl and grumbling infuriated her. Johan whimpered in her arms.

Bestemor reached for the boy. "He's right, child, dance with your classmate." She nudged Mari toward Leif. "Johan can dance with us."

The boy squirmed in Mari's arms until she put him down. He toddled off to his parents without looking back. Mari turned to Leif but heard a cry of pain. Bestemor was balancing on one foot and leaning heavily on Mrs. Nilsson's arm. Mari grabbed one arm and Leif the other, and the two helped her sit.

"My ankle. I twisted my ankle. Owww . . ."

Mari knelt to examine it, but the doctor stepped in. He probed and started to unlace her boot.

Bestemor waved him aside and stood up. "Not here. Just get me home."

Leif took her elbow and insisted on helping before anyone else could.

"I can manage alone," Mari said, sliding her grandma's arm over one shoulder. When she wrapped her own arm around Bestemor's tiny waist, she thought she might even be able to carry her.

"Nonsense, let the boy help us." Bestemor brushed aside the others who offered help. "Stay and enjoy the music. I'm in good hands with these strong young people."

Bestemor clung to Leif's arm, and Mari decided not to fight them both, but insisted on supporting her grandmother on the slow, careful walk home.

Once Bestemor was settled on the sofa with ice on her ankle, Leif ignored Mari's hints to leave.

"You don't want to miss your celebration, do you?" Mari asked. She thought she had kept the bitterness out of her voice, but the look on her grandma's face told her she failed.

"There's plenty of time to share a little news first." He plopped down on the sofa and began jabbering away about the latest progress of Hitler's troops in Russia and Africa.

Mari wracked her brain for excuses to make him leave.

Bestemor interrupted her thoughts. "Leif, you always know so much more than the rest of us. You should be a radio announcer."

Mari recognized the old woman's hint that details Leif was sharing weren't generally available and she should appear more interested in his updates. Otherwise he could suspect them of getting BBC news. It might even be a trick to see what they knew.

Mari forced her face into an expression of curiosity and surprise as he rattled off details she had heard the night before.

He stayed for almost an hour. Then, finally, his litany offered *real* news.

Shocking news.

Soldiers were coming to collect pet dogs in two weeks. A select unit of trainers would arrive to take and prepare healthy dogs for military service. Leif told them he had seen posters showing dogs as messengers and camp guards. This would free soldiers to fight, he said.

All dog owners in the village would be required to report to the train station where their pets would be examined, tested, and crated for travel. They needed young, strong, smart dogs; ones who followed orders.

In two weeks!

Thor was nearing two years old; he was smart, strong, and healthy. The worst part was that Per had trained him to sit and stay when soldiers approached and to follow orders instantly. After what happened to Odin, they couldn't risk having Thor react to the Germans as enemies or try to protect Astrid. Thor weighed only eighteen kilos, but he was all muscle and could outrun rabbits.

They would take him in a minute!

When Leif finally left, Bestemor unlaced her boot and showed Mari that her ankle was fine; it had all been a ruse to avoid the dancing. She told Mari to wait for the celebration to end, then hurry to tell Astrid and Per about the dog recruitment. They needed to come up with a plan to save Thor.

The posters went up a week later. But by then Mari, Astrid, and Per had cooked up a strategy to protect Thor.

Ytre Arna had few animals suitable for the Germans.

When food rationing had begun, most younger outdoor dogs had been sent away to live with relatives on farms in other districts. Most of the dogs still in town were too small or too old to be used. Others had trouble running because of injuries. The Germans wanted outdoor working dogs, healthy and fit. Thor was sure to be chosen.

The solution they came up with was *nearly* perfect. Astrid's grandparents lived on rich farmland in South Trondelag, in the lowlands near the Trondheim Fjord. It was a place where a dog could live well, but easily be hidden from German snoops. For now, the Nazi order only applied to dogs in the coastal districts, so Thor should be safe on their inland farm where he could be justified as a working dog. Astrid would move there to help her grandparents. Per could make the journey with her, then stay on as a farm hand.

There was one hurdle to such a perfect plan, though. A huge one. Quisling's rules from earlier in the year were still enforced. Travel across district lines required a special pass, approved by Gestapo headquarters. It could take months to get approval. And even with passes, they wouldn't be allowed to take Thor, not now.

Somehow they needed to sneak him away with them. And it had to happen soon.

Papa was having false papers made, but they might not be ready in time.

Putting their heads together, Doctor Olsen and Mari developed an alternative approach, but it was risky.

Chapter Thirty-Three

Gone but not Forgotten

December, 1942

At two o'clock on Saturday all registered dogs were at the station. The forged passes hadn't arrived in time. There was no choice but to put their back-up plan into action.

Earlier in the week, for several days, the doctor had dispensed what he calculated should be the exact doses of drugs needed to disable Thor, but only temporarily. The poor dog had a hard time standing and walking, or even swallowing. His tongue lolled out of his mouth.

Thor didn't know what was wrong and wobbled about, whining. It broke their hearts to see, but the doctor said Thor wasn't in pain and should recover quickly.

They adjusted his medication until he was able to walk, but he was uncoordinated and weak. Astrid coaxed him on slow walks through town during this period so the changes in him would be noticed. Meanwhile, Mrs.

Tomasson had been asking for advice from everyone at work, saying that Thor must have gotten into something poisonous or perhaps ate a sick animal.

When Saturday arrived about a dozen people reported with their dogs, including two dogs Mari had never seen before. Those two were both young and healthy and were taken immediately. The man who brought them walked off with a fistful of ration tickets. What kind of person would hand over his dogs for a few extra meals?

The officer in charge sent the smallest dogs home, along with old and disabled ones.

Thor displayed his good training and did his best to follow their commands. He sat and came when called. But he couldn't stand steady for long, he couldn't run, and he responded to their commands very slowly.

A Gestapo officer, one everyone called Walrus, was furious. He blustered and fumed. "What's wrong with him? He's the best *Hund* in town. What have you done to him?" He glared with suspicion at Astrid, and then at Per and Mari in turn.

Astrid recited her well-rehearsed story. "We don't know. He probably ate something on the mountainside. Maybe a dead animal that had a disease." She hugged Thor's neck. "He's been a little better today."

The soldiers began moving away the crated dogs. Walrus was disappointed not to add the prized spitz. He commanded Astrid to bring Thor back on Monday. "That's two days from now. If this animal recovers by then, he will join the others and be very useful to the Führer's cause."

His voice was sharp. "These men are off to collect more *Hunde* in Garnes, Indre Arna, and Fana. They'll return Monday and you will, too, at the same time."

Mari, Per, and Astrid helped Thor make the long walk home.

To their disappointment, no traveling passes arrived that night. Time was running out.

Papa delivered the forged passes Sunday night. They identified Per and Astrid correctly, but the reason for travel was false, as were the signatures. There was a forged letter, too, apparently signed by a German commander in that district, claiming that farm help was needed locally.

Astrid and Per had packed for a long stay, saying private goodbyes as soon as the passes arrived. Greta's father gave them a list of people along the route who would provide safe shelter at curfew times or if they had to wait out extreme weather.

Snow cover was light so early in the year, but they had figured out a way to keep Thor secret on the long journey. Papa had modified a wagon-sled to make a hidden compartment, and Doctor Olsen was confident the drugs Thor had taken would wear off enough that he could travel.

Mari had been working with the spitz since Sunday night. She massaged his muscles to work out the old drugs. He was recovering quickly.

No one was sure if their plan would work, but all agreed it was worth the risk.

By midday on Monday, Thor's symptoms had almost disappeared. As the last step in their preparations, Mari gave him a strong sedative before she left on her own to meet the soldiers. Poor Thor became very sleepy and couldn't even get up on his feet by the time she left.

The soldiers were surprised when only Mari showed up at the train station.

"Where is the *Hund?*" Walrus demanded, his mustache bristling with anger.

"He couldn't come. He's much worse. See for yourselves if you must."

When Mrs. Tomasson opened the door at the Nilsson house, Astrid was on the floor with Thor, weeping. She cradled him like a baby. One soldier tried to pull him to his feet, but he was as limp as a dead mackerel. The Germans left in disgust, without examining him closely. They didn't want to touch a sick dog.

As soon as they were gone, Mari injected Thor with a mild stimulant and massaged his legs and back. In just an hour, the dog was on his feet and moving steadily. He wasn't back to full strength, but he could drink water and looked more like the Thor they knew, although a little bleary-eyed.

Mari complimented Astrid's performance for the soldiers. "Your tears even had me convinced Thor was dying, and I know better."

"I just pictured them taking him away from me, and tears came easily. That's all I thought about while you were gone." She pulled Thor into a hug and kissed the top of his head.

Astrid's bundles were larger than Per's. Per had grown enough that he'd be able to wear farm clothes left behind by Astrid's uncles, who were off in the mountains with the resistance troops.

Mari gave Astrid several items of clothing and a sturdy pair of shoes she had outgrown. Mama had held them back for bartering, but Astrid needed them more now, and would have a hard time finding such things in the countryside.

"Can you sew?" Mari asked as she was helping her friend pack. "These will need to be refitted for you, but the fabrics are in good shape. I'm getting pretty good at that, but I won't be there to help."

"Oh my, yes. Living with Mama, Mrs. Jensen, and Mrs. Nilsson left me no choice. Every time one of them mends or alters or applies a fancy stitch, it's 'Astrid, come and let me show you how to do this.' I can probably barter my sewing skills for ration tickets if soldiers need repairs."

Their laughter was genuine, but tinged with nerves.

Mari hugged her friend and added, "I'm not giving you any sweaters. Those I can always take apart and reknit. You'll have to befriend the Trondelag sheep so they'll share their wool with you."

Per's and Mari's fathers loaded the wagon and fastened all the bags and bundles securely.

Mari gave Thor a final hug while her friends said goodbye to their families. Then the doctor tucked Thor in his hidden compartment, and Mari hugged her two best friends one last farewell.

"I'm going to miss all three of you so much. But it's a relief not to see Thor taken by the Germans. Be careful, be strong, and take care of each other." Mari struggled to blink back the tears burning her eyes.

Per gripped her wrist and guided her a few steps away. With his back to the others, he reached inside his jacket and pulled out the ledger, pressing it into her hands. His head dipped close to hers so no one else would hear. "I've done the best I could to write a few things for Bjorn, but now it's up to you. He wants to know about his village, not sheep and pigs and harvests."

Mari hugged it for a moment, wishing it could be Bjorn himself in her arms. Then she pushed it back into Per's hands. "After you told me about this, guess what? I began writing to Bjorn in my own notebooks."

She added with a grin. "Don't worry, I have a safe place to keep my words out of German hands."

"So what should I do with this? You could hide it with yours."

"Nei, nei, you take it. Keep writing. The Germans have penetrated every corner of our country, so every story needs to be told. I have no doubt you'll continue fighting them in your clever ways. There will be things to report, even in farm country. Write about that."

She noted his shoulders straighten and a smile brightened his face.

Mari continued. "Every voice must be heard when Norway is finally ours again. Bjorn will have his stories to tell, and when it is all pieced together, the truth will be stronger than all the Nazi lies."

"I'll do my best." Per slipped his arms out of his heavy rucksack, opened it, and maneuvered the ledger into a slim seam near the bracings. After tucking a flap back in place, the ledger appeared to be part of the pack itself.

"That should do it, even if border guards search us." He lowered his voice further. "If they do find it, I've been very careful about the way I worded things, using code names, as Bjorn instructed."

He patted the side of his rucksack and added, "I'm taking Bjorn's carving with me, too. It sounds a little crazy, but it makes me feel like Bjorn is not so far away. It helps me remember every bit of advice he ever shared."

Mari nodded and patted his arm. While Per shouldered his pack and returned to the sled, the bustle of final arrangements pulled Mari back to the danger her friends were facing.

It was time. Amid last-minute hugs and farewells, handshakes and reminders, Astrid and Per pushed off, eager to reach their first stop before curfew.

In some ways Mari wanted to go with them, but she didn't envy their days of winter travel pushing a loaded sled, especially with a not-so-tiny dog hidden under the seat. Nor would she welcome being stopped by patrolling Germans and district guards.

Astrid's sock held enough sedatives to keep Thor sleeping through longer stretches of travel, but at a much milder dose. If all went well, they'd arrive at the farm within a week and Thor would be safe.

Now all she could do was wait to hear that they had arrived.

Chapter Thirty-Four

Friend or Foe, Again

Knowing that her two friends were gone and not likely to return until the war ended ripped a painful hole in Mari's heart. Even writing to them was out of the question, at least for a good while, because of the censors. Mari didn't want to tip off the authorities that her friends had traveled north, as their passes were not authentic ones.

Mari returned the next morning to her notebook of unposted letters to her brother. Per's reminder of Bjorn's advice to use coded language led her to reread all that she had written. When she did, her initial panic about keeping a journal returned. The seclusion of the attic had lulled her into a false sense of safety.

She had used real names, describing secrets too freely. Her family had managed to harbor the British soldier and Rachel's family without being caught. But what if the writings were discovered? Long after those escapes were safely accomplished, her own words could provide evidence to justify her arrest and that of her father, mother, and Bestemor, too.

As she sat on the carpet, notebook on her lap, her thoughts drifted to memories of Rachel's family and Bernie. How long would it be before she would learn what happened to them?

How long before the people she cared for most would return home, safe and sound? When would she see Astrid and Per again? And Bjorn?

Her letters drew her closer to Bjorn, reminding her of far greater risks he was taking. He believed in her, counted on her. He would have agreed with her insistence to Per to tell his stories, too, to make every effort to record the truth.

But would Bjorn even survive to read her words? In a tiny corner of her mind she dared to ask the question: If not, was it worth the risk to everyone she loved to keep writing? Somehow, she felt that Bjorn knew she had been writing to him, as silly as that might sound to anyone else.

At the same time, Mari felt that he would understand if she quit writing and destroyed her words.

For several minutes she was tempted to burn her notebooks. It would be easy to do in Bestemor's fireplace.

Instead, she chose to continue.

Setting the notebook aside she dropped through the hatch and returned in moments. She couldn't stand the idea of giving up, of giving in to the power and terror the Germans tried to wield. She had survived greater loss and fear when Odin was killed, and she would count on him now to give her courage.

She set Bjorn's carving of Odin on the carpet at her side, and wrote.

She wrote about the Germans collecting dogs. Then she added more about Astrid and Per leaving for Trondelag to help on the farm. However, she avoided describing details of Thor's escape.

When she finished, she covered Odin's carving with the skein of yarn in the small footstool, leaving him to guard her words.

The headcount at the house was up to fourteen soldiers. The Germans grumbled constantly about the overcrowding. What would they say if they had to live as Rachel and the girls did for five weeks?

And then there was that thorn in her foot, Leif.

The very day he heard that Per and Astrid were gone, he had caught up with Mari after school. She forced herself to let him walk and talk with her, but before they were halfway to the cottage, her head was throbbing.

"I was sorry to hear that Thor died, Mari." Leif kept chattering, trying to engage her in his one-sided conversation. "He was a handsome dog, and smart, too. At least it wasn't the soldiers who killed this one."

She fumed at his comments, but at the same time was relieved to know he had accepted the rumors as truth.

Mrs. Nilsson did a splendid job spreading their story: Thor died in Astrid's arms; it broke the little girl's heart; she accepted a long-standing invitation from her grandparents to live with them in the country; she couldn't travel alone, so Per joined her to help her grandparents on their farm.

Leif had swallowed the rumors completely and then twisted the story to suit his own beliefs. "Astrid may have needed to go, but Per left because he's a coward. He jumped at any excuse to run away. If he knows what's good for him, he'll stay there, too."

Mari clamped her jaws tighter.

When she didn't answer, Leif pushed harder. "Per was a troublemaker. If he stayed, he'd have ended up in jail. I've never understood why you like him so much."

She sputtered, "Because he's a friend, Leif. I trust him. Astrid, too." Then she squeezed her lips tight before she said more.

He stepped back as if she'd slapped him.

They walked on in silence until they neared Mari's gate. He took her arm to stop her. When she tried to twist free, his grip tightened. "Face it, Mari. I'm the only friend you've got now. You spend all your time with old and sick people. You're hardly ever at school anymore. Use those brains of yours. Count on me to take care of you, and stop acting so superior."

She did her best to keep a stone face, to mask the fury that threatened to spill out in words. He of all people had no right to judge what she did with her days. But he had an aggravating knack for sprinkling bits of truth into his rants. She *had* wrapped her studies and her medical work around her like a cocoon, hoping she wouldn't have to emerge until the war was over.

She missed her friends already.

She longed to be a normal schoolgirl.

Leif released her arm when it was clear she wouldn't answer him. "Think about what I said, Mari. I could do you a lot of good, and you'd have someone your own age to talk to. Is that such a bad thing?"

It was almost frightening how well he recognized her unspoken thoughts.

Having someone her own age to talk with, to laugh with, would be such a relief.

But not Leif.

Never Leif.

He trotted across the road and Mari spent the next hour sipping tea and massaging her temples.

And thinking about what he said.

Chapter Thirty-Five

Jul Joy with Lise

Lise came home for just one night on the Saturday before Jul, after spending the previous week with Erik and his family. She would leave for a week's duty at a hospital in Bergen the next day.

Once again she played the role of the Jule Nisse, delivering a few delicious treasures for them. The harvest on the farm that year had been better with Erik's help, but the Germans, of course, were demanding more from all the farms in the district. Lise said there was reason for their greed. More than 200,000 soldiers now occupied "Fortress Norway." The Germans were well-fed while rations for Norwegians were reduced month by month.

Mama had the evening off. Many soldiers would spend the night partying in town, while a few took the train to Bergen for holiday celebrations. Mari's family welcomed the luxury of an early supper and long conversation, a chance to relax and catch up on news.

Lise wrapped her hands around her empty cup, and welcomed Mari's offer of hot water. "It's still hard for me to see you as old enough to handle boiling water, little one. Each time I come I notice more changes in you."

She gestured to Mari to sit down and join them, reaching for her hand. "When I left for University, you were only eight. Just look at you now. You're hiding spies and runaway families, rescuing Thor, and saving lives with the doctor."

Mari blushed and squeezed Lise's hand. The lull in conversation felt awkward, but she didn't know what to say.

Papa took a long draw on his pipe and patted Mari's other hand. "Every day I marvel at how grown our baby girl has become."

Mari changed the subject. "How are things going for Erik and his family?"

Lise's stories provided some of the heartiest laughs of the night.

Although German troops were concentrated on the coastlines, they had started demanding housing in the midlands so they could keep an eye on farm production. No soldiers moved in with Erik's family, though, because word of his "illness" spread faster than measles.

Lise shared a story about a local patrol trying to install two soldiers with some elderly neighbors. The little old woman refused. Instead, she took a pair of brooms and blocked the path to her door. Lise said the snowy top of her head barely reached the officer's chest, but she marched right up to him, stamped her feet, and waved the brooms in his face, shouting, "Over my dead body!" The German officer blustered and scolded, but he left with his patrol and never returned.

Bestemor nearly fell off her chair in a rush to grab two brooms and prop her "weapons" near the door!

Lise's reports continued. Some Germans were stationed in the farm regions to search for resistance spies. Others were there, she said, to supervise Russian prisoners, brought to Norway to serve in forced labor camps. Lise said those prisoners were lucky, because even farm scraps were better than the food they would get in prisons in Germany.

Lise said one job the prisoners were given was to plaster German slogans, posters, and propaganda on every surface. She told how one prisoner was ordered to paint *WORK FOR NEW NORWAY* along the sides of bridges. He claimed he was confused about exactly where to place the letters and painted the slogan on the foundations as close to the ground as possible. After that, farmers stopped at bridges to rest their horses, secretly unloading forkfuls of manure at the base of the signs. In a very short time the signs were unreadable.

The laughs from Lise's stories were as satisfying as the stash of foods she revealed. But best of all was a surprise she saved for last. At the end of the meal, Lise went back to her case and returned to lay a small bundle on the table. She unfolded a sweater.

Inside was a carved bear!

Mari recognized Bjorn's work instantly. The whole family knew at once what it was. She passed it around, and each member of the family took a turn to examine it up close, as they pounded Lise with questions.

"Erik has a pass to travel around his district to work on farm equipment. The German authorities are happy to have him do that, but they avoid him, because of his rumored disease. So, he travels freely on his own schedule. Not long ago he saw this carving in a farmer's home. It had been traded for food and clothing just days before Erik was there."

Mari was unable to breathe for several moments when she heard that.

They all looked again at the carving. It was of a powerful bear standing on an eagle's neck.

"It was proudly displayed in their home, because the farmer recognized the message in the design: Norway will stamp out the Nazis. When Erik looked at it closely he noticed something important and declared he had to have it. The farmer bartered hard, but Erik offered additional days of labor, which sealed the deal."

When it was Mari's turn to hold the polished wood piece, she touched every surface, then flipped it over to see the familiar signature on the base. As she expected, it was carved with the letter *B* and a paw print.

Below that was etched: *Nov-42.*

"Bjorn completed this just last month—November 1942!"

Hands reached for it, each one wanting another turn to see the marks.

"He has never dated pieces before." Mama wiped at her eyes and gripped Papa's hands. "Do you think that's what it means?"

Mari didn't wait to hear his reply.

"Yes, of course that's what it means," Mari said. "He's alive, and still here in Norway!"

When the carving came around to her again, she held on to it for the longest time, slowly stroking the finely carved fur of the wooden bear, lost in thought, delighted to hold something Bjorn had touched so recently.

What a Christmas miracle. If only for one night, it felt as if they were all reunited as a family.

Chapter Thirty-Six

Uninvited Guest

As soon as Lise left on Sunday, Mama and Bestemor began preparing the soldiers' German holiday recipes. Somehow all the impossible-to-find necessary ingredients had been delivered to the house. The captain in charge scheduled their Christmas Eve meal for early afternoon so the men could go into town or to Bergen that night.

Early on the morning of Julaften, Mama and Bestemor left the house to prepare the soldiers' dinner feast before Mari was awake. As soon as the soldiers' meal was served and the kitchen was cleaned, they would be free to leave for their own celebration.

Mrs. Nilsson had invited Mari's family and Doctor Olsen to celebrate Julaften supper with them. Her home was small, but not as tiny as the cottage. It had the added advantage of not having soldiers and NS members for neighbors. Mari's spirits bubbled at the prospect of spending Christmas Eve with those she trusted most.

A few weeks earlier, Mr. Jensen had recovered enough

from his imprisonment to move out of the doctor's home and into Mrs. Nilsson's house. His mother was thrilled to have him home. He was gradually getting his strength back and wanted to teach again, but the Gestapo wouldn't let him return to school. They said it would be "disruptive."

He had recovered enough to help with chores, and his stories were always entertaining. He didn't talk about what happened at the camp, but his poor health revealed the consequences of his loyalty to the king. It could be months or even years before the full effects faded. Mari had no doubt that some memories would be with him forever.

Mari was still waiting to learn of Astrid and Per's safe arrival at the farm. Mari missed her friend nearly as much as Astrid's mother did. Thankfully, Mrs. Nilsson had received messages from families along the way where the pair and pup had stayed overnight during the first days. It seemed that their passes had been accepted at the district crossings. Mari hoped the lack of letters after that meant Astrid was just avoiding attention from the mail censors.

On the morning before Jul, as soon as she got out of bed, Mari was busy in Bestemor's cottage.

She hurried through dusting and cleaning, then started to iron fresh clothing and aprons for that evening. They couldn't wear bunad, of course, but that didn't mean they shouldn't look their best. While she worked, she hummed Jul songs and savored the scent from the little spruce sapling Papa propped in a place of honor on the coffee table.

There would be no room for a big *Juletre*—a grand, spreading Christmas tree—in the little cottage.

Her gaze lingered on Bjorn's carving. Setting the iron aside, she moved Bjorn's bear carving from the mantle to a perfect spot under the miniature tree.

When everything was in place for the evening, she realized she had time to write a quick Jul greeting to Bjorn.

Her note to Bjorn was brief, just a Jul wish and a promise to write more the next day. Mari slid the notebook into place and covered Odin's carving with the yarn. She was on the last page of her second notebook and would begin another for the New Year.

As her foot touched the pantry floor, she remembered how sparse the evening supper would be compared to other holidays. She tossed her coat around her shoulders and hurried across the yard to the storage shelves in the cellar of the main house.

A long, unpredictable winter lay ahead, but one jar of preserves could be spared to make the meal more festive. She debated taking a small jar of golden cloudberries or a large jar of blueberries. Blueberries were abundant, so were not as prized as other fruits. But with so many sharing the meal, she realized the larger jar would provide more generous servings, making her decision easy.

When she swung open the cellar door again to return to the cottage, she nearly dropped the precious preserves.

Across the yard, Goatman stood on the cottage doorstep, his hand on the knob. He must have heard Mari's startled gasp because he spun around and then quickly stepped off the porch.

Mari's instinct was to run back into the cellar and pull the door shut after her, but anger and curiosity anchored her to the spot.

"*Guten tag, Fräulein.* No laundry on Christmas Eve, is there?" He seemed fully recovered from his initial surprise as he approached her. His thin lips barely moved when he spoke, but his projecting jaw worked itself sideways once or twice after the words stopped, a habit accented by his scrawny chin-beard and flat nose with wide nostrils. His nickname was one of the easiest to choose, and the more she saw of him, the more it suited him.

"*Guten tag. Nein,* I came for this." She clutched the jar against her chest and straightened her spine to appear as tall and confident as possible. She wanted to rush past him, but kept her feet firmly planted on the top step of the cellar. She was determined not to leave until he did.

His eyes darted back to the cottage. "I thought your mother was home, but I see she is not."

Mari held the preserves like a shield. "Nei, she is not. She is cooking in the main house."

She looked up at the main house and saw Mama through the large window above the kitchen sink. Bestemor was just beyond her, rolling dough at the table. Goatman must be able to see them there as easily as she did. Why had he been trying to open the door to the cottage?

Mari nodded toward the house, adding. "She's right where you'd expect her to be, don't you see?"

His chin twitched again, and his eyes darted to the house window and back to the cottage door. He muttered something Mari recognized as German cursing and shuffled his weight from foot to foot, but Mari's feet stayed firmly planted.

In a few moments he took his twitching chin, foul language, and grumbling to the house. She kept her eyes locked on his back, noting that he turned to check on her more than once before clicking the kitchen door shut behind him.

When Goatman was gone, Mari set the jar of preserves carefully on the stone path and reached for the heavy cellar door. Not since she was ten years old was the weight of it more than she could handle, but this time it slipped through her shaking fingers and slammed shut the last few inches. She fastened the latch and picked up the jar.

She walked slowly across the yard, putting one foot in front of the other, taking each breath deeply and slowly before exhaling. By the time she unlocked the cottage and put her coat on the hook behind the door, she had calmed down considerably. She relocked the door and hung the key on the hook near the mantel. Whatever Goatman was after, she had returned just in time to disrupt his plans. She set the jar to take with them that evening under the pine sapling on the table.

That's when she noticed it.

Bjorn's carving was lying on its side.

She *knew* it wasn't that way when she left. She *had* locked the door, and it was locked when she returned. She took a quick tour of the tiny cottage to reassure herself that she was alone. Then she double-checked the door to make sure it was locked.

Mari was tempted to race to the house and report her suspicions to the captain of the German squad. Bestemor said Goatman was not well-liked by the other soldiers and was often blamed for taking their things. Maybe the unit leader would send him away!

Then Mari remembered Papa's warning to stay as far away from Goatman as possible. He was said to be a specialist at tracing radio signals and tracking down spies, although it sounded like he had not been very successful so far. Even if his own soldiers didn't like him, they'd never send away such a valuable asset, based on the complaint of a young Norwegian girl that the man was behaving oddly. All she would do is make him into more of an enemy than he already was.

Mari decided to wait until after the holiday to tell her parents and Bestemor about what happened and her concerns about Goatman. In the meantime she would increase her vigilance about locks and using the attic.

Mari was dressed and waiting for the others to return home. She lined a basket with one of Bestemor's finest Jul cloths and packed it with a generous share of Lise's bounty and the preserves. She saved space for any leftover holiday treats sent home with Mama and Bestemor.

Even when meals were meager, her family never failed to give thanks for the food they were served. Mari looked forward to robust echoes of "*Takk for maten*" at the table that evening. The traditional "Thank you for the food" at the end of a meal was no longer just a courteous habit. These days, they were truly thankful for every morsel.

She had allowed a place in the basket for Bestemor's homemade akevitt. Mari couldn't begrudge her grandma the potatoes to make alcohol, not since she witnessed the relief it offered when Bestemor had been in pain two years ago.

On her rounds through the village, many asked if Mari had brought pain relief treatments. But ice and iodine were all Mari had to offer. If a patient needed more, she followed the doctor's lead and looked the other way if they took a few sips of liquor for added comfort.

It was a puzzle how her grandma managed to make akevitt—and where she hid it, considering their cramped circumstances. Still, Mari had no doubt that a bottle would appear before they left for their celebration.

Next she arranged her personal gifts in a tote: hats for Papa, the doctor, and Mr. Jensen, and mittens for the ladies. She used the yarn from her outgrown sweaters, socks, and two old scarves to knit new items with colors and patterns chosen individually. She set aside the little sweater she made for Johan to deliver on Jul morning.

Footsteps on the cottage stoop alerted her for the sound of Papa's key in the lock.

Instead she heard a knock.

Would Goatman really dare to return? Would he knock?

She peeked under a blackout curtain to see who it was.

Leif.

He spotted her at the window, smiled and waved. She couldn't pretend she wasn't home.

When she unlocked and opened the door, he picked up a wooden box and carried it in. "*God Jul*, Mari!"

"God Jul to you, but what is this about, Leif?"

He walked past her and set the box on the table. "It's a holiday gift. Uncle Frederick and Tante Helene received a generous basket from the mayor and wanted to share the joy of the season with their neighbors."

While he spoke he unloaded items on the table: chunks of cheese, a half kilo of butter, a jar of honey, a small tin of ham, a large tin of crackers, dried fruits, and a small cloth bag tied with twine. He tossed the bag up and down in his palm and said, "Guess what this is. *Nei*, you'll never guess. It's COFFEE!"

The sight of so many foods that had once been commonplace but were now luxuries nearly took her breath away. It should have made her mouth water, but instead her tongue was as dry as wool flannel. How could he possibly think she would accept this?

"Mari, are you home? Why is this door unlocked?"

Her father crossed to the kitchen in a few strides, his coat still on. He looked nearly as worried as he did when she asked about the British agent.

"I'm sorry, Papa. Leif was just leaving—and taking his gifts with him." She began repacking the box while Papa locked the door and hung up his coat.

"God Jul, Leif. We wish you the blessings of the season. Now what's this all about?" He watched Mari pack the last chunk of cheese and hand the box to Leif.

Leif took the box from Mari without argument and extended it to her father. "God Jul to you and your family, sir. Your daughter may not wish to accept these, but they are a gift to all of you, so it's not her choice."

Leif's smile was wide, and he spoke with confidence and charm. "It's from Uncle Frederick and Tante Helene, sharing some of their bounty with their neighbors. Enjoy!"

He pushed the box into her father's arms and stepped back. Papa looked from Leif to Mari to the box in silence.

Mari was unable to read his face, but she assumed he was as appalled at the idea as she was.

Leif spoke again more gently. "Please. Why not enjoy some very scarce items when you have the chance? If you don't take it, I'm to deliver it to the soldiers. From what I've seen they have more than enough indulgences to fill their bellies."

He looked from Mari to her father and back to Mari.

"Can't you see that I'm trying to offer you a little holiday comfort?"

Papa still said nothing, and Mari was waiting for him to signal their refusal. Leif edged toward the door.

Papa set the box on the table and then put one hand on Leif's shoulder. Mari could hardly believe what she was seeing or hearing.

"Thank your aunt and uncle for us, if you will. These gifts are very generous, and we'll appreciate having them." Papa opened the door, extending his hand to the tall, blond-haired young fellow. "God Jul, Leif. It was kind of you to think of us."

They shook hands.

As Leif stepped outside, he caught Mari's stunned gaze, smiled, and called out, "God Jul to you all."

Mari struggled to sound as sincere as Papa as she called back, "God Jul to you too, Leif."

Chapter Thirty-Seven

Family and Friends

The Julaften party was a surprisingly traditional Christmas Eve gathering for such hard times. Using Lise's gifts and the bountiful contents of Leif's box, they were able to set a deliciously full *smorgasbord.* Mari pitched in with the chattering women, laying out Mrs. Nilsson's festive table runners, china and linens, and even crystal glasses for their toasts.

"Your dishes are elegant, Mrs. Nilsson." Mari adjusted the plates to make room for the napkins.

"Takk, they're from my wedding. I love them. If this war struggles on much longer, I'll have to barter them away eventually. It's a joy to share them with all of you on such a happy occasion."

"This reminds me of Lise's wedding day," Mari noted.

Bestemor slipped an arm around her waist and said, "I was thinking the same thing, little one. But this time we even have the aroma of coffee brewing!"

Smiles in the crowded kitchen stretched wall to wall.

The men in attendance wouldn't have had room to

help with the preparations if they tried, but Mr. Jensen called from the parlor that they would do the dishes afterward.

His mother shook her head vigorously. "Nei, takk, Magnus. You've broken most of mine over the years. I won't let you break Elsa's beautiful heirlooms."

When the laughter subsided Mrs. Nilsson said, "You should have trained him better, Oliva. Both of my boys washed these very dishes and not one of them has a chip or a rough edge."

Papa's voice came from the parlor. "Your dishes may be perfect, Elsa, but the last I saw those boys of yours, especially Olav, they had some rough edges!"

Laughter and light filled the house and lasted throughout the evening with few thoughts of what was happening beyond the blackout curtains.

Before the meal began, each glass held a serving of akevitt. Doctor Olsen led them in the familiar prayer of grace, and then, one by one, they wished a *God Jul* and *Glade Nytt År* to those not at the table.

Lise, Erik, and Bjorn. Astrid and Per. Olav and Lars. Even Thor.

Then, the names of other loved ones, living and dead, were added, each staying in their thoughts and prayers for a few moments.

Mari's few words about Odin caught in her throat. After that she held silent, thinking about those whose names she didn't dare speak aloud: Bernie, Rachel, Eva, Gilda.

She added a silent prayer for the other Jewish friends and neighbors who were gone from the village: Mr. Meier, and Sarah and her family.

When the time came to lift their heads and their glasses, Mari saw red eyes and somber faces. Bestemor noticed, too.

She raised her glittering crystal glass. "If my akevitt can't make our wishes come true, nothing can! *Skoal!*" She tipped her glass and downed the contents in one swallow.

"Skoal!" was heard all around the table, following her lead.

Mari had a small bit in a glass, too, but knew better than to gulp Bestemor's improvised alcohol. She sipped, swallowed, and wondered if this throat-burning concoction relieved pain or just replaced it.

Mrs. Nilsson gasped, but lifted her glass again. "Save one sip, there's someone I've forgotten." Glasses were raised, and faces around the table looked curious.

"To Alf, who warms my feet and my soul. What would I do without you, my old friend?"

"To Alf!" The crowded dining room resounded with laughter as the last drops of alcohol were consumed.

Mari peeked under the table and saw the ancient cat had wrapped himself around Mrs. Nilsson's ankles, settling in to wait for the inevitable treats that would come his way as the evening progressed.

Small dabs of each offering filled their plates to overflowing. Belts and apron ties were loosened. Mari counted this as one of the most memorable and delicious suppers of her short life. If the time ever came when Norway returned to the way it was before the invasion, she promised to always remember what a precious gift it was to have enough to eat and more to share with others.

She had to admit that without Leif's extras, it would have been difficult to fill everyone's plates.

The doctor passed around a small pouch of German tobacco he received after treating a prominent NS member. The men tamped it into the bowls of their pipes and drew deeply on the smoke.

Bestemor patted the doctor's hand. "Takk for sharing your luxuries. If you men stuffed your pipes with the usual stinkweed tonight, it would ruin the delicious aromas of our banquet."

"I'm happy to share, Dagmar. The scarcity of tobacco has been good for my lungs, because I can't stand the substitutes either." He nodded toward the men and asked, "You don't taste any German in this tobacco, do you?"

Mari listened to their banter while she washed dishes. She pondered the doctor's willingness to offer his medical expertise to all villagers, regardless of their attitudes toward the Germans. Local NS members were welcomed by German doctors at Nazi headquarters and could get medications easily. Even so, many preferred seeing Doctor

Olsen and often paid him generously, including bonuses like tobacco.

If he refused to care for Nazi supporters, they wouldn't go untreated. At first Mari resented his choices, but gradually her opinion was changing. These were people he had known for a lifetime. The doctor treated everyone like family. If he benefited from extra income, he put it to good use helping others in desperate need. Her family was doing the same with Mama's work benefits. That very night, Papa's decision to accept Leif's gifts had helped them all.

Those choices felt wrong in some ways, but right in others. Mari struggled with her conscience, recognizing that few things in life had the precise answers of mathematics or science.

She found her thoughts drifting to encounters with Leif. How could she decide when to accept a gift or kindness from someone like that and when to uphold an "ice front"? What choice was or wasn't right?

When she finished in the kitchen, Mari served freshly brewed coffee, then she fetched her backpack.

"I don't mean to interrupt," she said, "but the Jule Nisse asked me to deliver some things. The early curfews are complicating their lives, too."

The *oohs* and *ahhs* of the items her knitting needles had produced caused her to blush. Each gift was modeled and admired, followed by warm hugs and "*Tusen Takk*s."

When the fuss died down, Mrs. Tomasson spoke up.

"Your mittens are warm and welcome, Mari. I hope you'll forgive me for saying it, but I received an even better gift this week. I want to share it with you tonight."

She pulled a letter out of her pocket. "It's from my parents in Trondelag. I'll read it aloud."

Carefully worded, the message first asked if everyone in Ytre Arna was fine and had enough to eat for the holidays. They were looking forward to better crops in the coming season. They mentioned how grateful they were that their "three young workers" were healthy and in good spirits.

It was a clear signal that Astrid, Per, and Thor had arrived safely. Mrs. Tomasson hugged Mari, delivering all the love meant for her absent daughter.

The friends lingered long, pausing at midnight for prayers and hymns, followed by snacking and storytelling. As the night rolled on, the topics turned to Hitler's recent setbacks and chances for an end to the war in the coming year. Mari enjoyed their hopeful predictions, but wondered if their optimistic views had been inflated by the plentiful food and akevitt. Could she dare to hope for Norway's freedom?

Eventually the doctor asked for his coat. "This has been a joyous night for me: the finest company, delicious food, and renewed hopes that Norway will be returned to us sooner rather than later." He moved from one to the next, kissing each woman's hand and offering deep bows to the gentlemen. "I have never said *Takk for maten* with a warmer heart or a more satisfied belly. *God Jul* to you, one and all."

Mari walked him to the door where he reminded her to sleep in the next day. "Clinic visits on Jul morning are unlikely, but I'm available if an emergency comes up." He hugged Mari and then Bestemor, who pressed a covered plate into his hands.

When the door clicked shut, Papa was holding Mama's coat for her.

Mr. Jensen helped Bestemor into her sleeves, and handed Mari her overcoat. After she slipped it on, he took Mari's hands in his. His bony fingers trembled but he spoke with the gentle, steady voice she remembered from the classroom.

"You are a remarkably talented young lady, Mari. Learning comes easily to you, and you've acquired knowledge and skills far beyond your years. The responsibilities you've shouldered are helping our entire village."

She blushed, but he held her hands and continued.

"Don't forget, skills can be gained by study, but wisdom is gained by living. And life's lessons are far more difficult, requiring many years of experience. You've taken on the role of an adult, but you're still a child. Allow yourself time to learn like a child, to observe and question and wonder. No one expects you to have all the answers."

She squeezed his hands and said, "I understand."

He tilted his head slightly, as he had often done in school. "Do you? I see the worries in your face, Mari. Life has always been complicated, but Hitler has turned it into a threatening labyrinth.

"Jewish scholars have studied their bible, the Torah, for centuries, and written about their thoughts in a book called the Talmud. One lesson the Talmud teaches is that the highest form of wisdom is kindness. This is perhaps the hardest lesson to understand, especially in difficult times like ours."

Mari wasn't surprised that Mr. Jensen knew about a Jewish book. She imagined that he knew something about every important book in the world.

He opened the door for her. "Let kindness be the lens through which you see everyone's choices, including your own. When you feel lost, don't be afraid to ask for help. I'll always be here for you."

Chapter Thirty-Eight

Star Bright, Jul Night

Mari's family climbed the gravel road to home under a waxing full moon. Papa's arm wrapped around Mama's shoulder, her head tucked against his chest. Clouds of frozen breath glittered like fairy dust in the crisp night air. He carried the basket with uneaten treasures that would stretch their celebration into Christmas Day.

Mari and Bestemor lagged behind. Curfew wasn't a worry that night because the soldiers had gone to Bergen or were celebrating in the village. Mari often needed reminders to shorten her stride when walking with her grandma, especially uphill. That night they strolled casually, arm-in-arm, a slow pace their unspoken collaboration. The luminous moonlight and aura of peace surrounding them were treasures to be savored.

When they finally swung open the gate, Bestemor pointed toward Mama who was already inside, peeking out past the corner of the blackout curtain. "Sonja will scold us both for staying out in the cold so long."

"Will she scold me, too, if I keep Mari outside a few minutes longer?"

Leif's voice startled Mari, but Bestemor broke into good-natured laughter. "You're a bit tall to be out helping the Jule Nisse, Leif."

She surprised Mari even more by tugging on his scarf, pulling him down for a gentle hug. "Takk for maten, Leif, and tusen takk to your aunt and uncle, too. Your generosity brightened our Jul celebration." She patted his arms and smiled up into his face, a smile that startled Mari with its apparent sincerity.

Leif bowed his head slightly and beamed. "I'll give them your thanks. It warms my heart to know that you enjoyed your holiday meal." He gripped the old woman's elbow and helped her up onto the stoop at the cottage door.

Mari was thoroughly annoyed at his intrusion. She was more than a little aggravated at Bestemor for treating him as some kind of a hero. Didn't she remember it was the Nazis who provided those goodies?

Mari lowered her head and approached the door, but Leif stepped into her path. "Please, Mari, will you stay behind a few minutes to talk? It's a beautiful night, and I have a question for you."

She shuffled several steps back rather than stand next to him. She wanted to glare into his eyes, the way she did with Goatman, but Leif was so tall she needed to create more distance between them.

"Can't it wait until tomorrow, Leif? It's cold and it's late. In fact, we're breaking curfew. Don't you have to report us to your German friends?"

She took more than a little satisfaction in seeing his smile fade. Just then the door opened, and light from inside the cottage cast shadows across Leif's face.

He gained an unexpected ally when Bestemor spoke up and said, "Tomorrow is Jul day, for the family, Mari. He's only asking for a few minutes."

Mama and Papa were at the door, waiting. Mama threw Mari a lifeline. "It's so cold and late. Won't it wait, Leif?"

But Papa chose that moment to contradict Mama, something Mari rarely witnessed. "Sonja, it's not so cold tonight, and not so very late. Let them have a few minutes to themselves."

Papa ushered Mama and Bestemor into the house. Before the door closed Papa added, "You did say a few minutes, right, Leif? We'll put a kettle on for tea, and I'll come for you when the water boils, if you care to join us."

Click.

Leif and Mari stood in the shadows.

Neither spoke.

Mari's mind raced, but she didn't dare to open her mouth. Let him ask his question. She'd answer him, and that would be that.

But his hand squeezed her elbow, guiding her to the

bench near the side of the cottage. It's no wonder he was well-liked by the soldiers—he was a natural at taking charge. She stiffened her shoulders, following his lead. Her teeth clenched, biting back a demand to spit out his question so she could go inside.

His mittened hand brushed light snow off the bench and he sat, patting the cleared space next to him. "Please, Mari, won't you join me? This won't take long, I promise."

She planned to remain standing, gaining a height advantage to glare at him. But the bench was bathed in a mixture of moonlight and starlight, nearly as bright as midday. Winter nights in Norway were incredibly long and so dark. Curfew eliminated any chance to bask in bright nights like this one. She sighed. She'd let him have his say while she soaked up the brilliant starry heavens.

She sat as far from him as she could and lifted her eyes toward the sky.

She felt Leif watching her, waiting for her to acknowledge him.

She didn't.

Finally, he spoke. "Mari, I apologize for calling Per a coward. He's always been a decent fellow, to me and to others. I know he didn't like me, but I do understand why you trust him."

That surprised Mari more than anything he had said or done so far. Should she believe him?

"You've known me just as long, and now that those two are gone, why must I be your enemy? Why won't you trust me as you trusted them? I could help you, protect you, be your friend again."

How could he think that would ever be possible?

Unlike Leif, Per had refused to join Unghird. He fought German propaganda with the resistance. If the Germans were still there when he was older, he'd probably join the mountain fighters, too.

She struggled to hold those thoughts inside, to wear an expression as blank as the moon's. She asked, "Why do you care what I think of you? You have plenty of Unghird friends."

Leif sighed, then continued. "The classes you take are with older students you barely know, and you avoid social events. Don't you ever want to just have some fun? If you'd let me I could help your family more often, like I did tonight. I could take you to some parties or dances and you could laugh and relax. Life could be easier for you. I've always liked your company."

How could she believe any of that? He made fun of her more than once, calling her a baby. He was acting as if an invasion had never happened. Her jaws ached from holding back her reply.

She locked her gaze onto the stars and clenched her fists inside her mittens, digging her fingernails into her palms. Angry outbursts in the past had caused too many problems, so she was determined not to provide him with evidence of her loyalty to Norway and its traditions.

They sat in silence for several minutes. If he thought

she was considering his offer, so be it. She could endure the awkward silence until Papa came to rescue her.

Suddenly Leif spoke again, this time with less bravado and confidence.

"Your silence says it all, Mari. You've erased any memory of me as the boy you grew up with. All you can see is my Unghird uniform. Can't you imagine, even for a minute, that I am still the boy you knew? I don't like seeing *anyone* hurt, least of all you and your family. I'm lonely, too, missing times when my life was less painful, less of a struggle."

That was more than Mari could ignore. "Really? Pain and struggle? Have you had an empty belly for even one day? Has your family's home or business been destroyed or stolen from you? You celebrate Nazi successes, turning your back on Norway's freedom and heritage. Then you dare to bargain for my friendship, offering privileges you gained from those decisions. How can you live with yourself after betraying Mr. Jensen?"

She was gripping the edge of the bench seat as she spoke, willing herself to stop, to regain control before she made things worse or endangered her family.

She was startled by Leif's outburst.

"Nei! Never!"

She saw the fury on his face.

"I never said a word against Mr. Jensen. I was asked, of course, about our teacher's loyalty, but no one was surprised when I said I'm a daydreamer, that I never paid much attention in class. Mr. Jensen did plenty to anger the Gestapo on his own, and that's what got him arrested. He didn't need reports from me. Your mind painted me as a villain, and your imagination filled in fantasy details without getting to the truth."

While he spoke he leaned toward her, and she felt blasted by the force of his denial.

Could that be true? After Mr. Jensen completed their class at Year Six, he worked with Year One students. Mari had feared he might not guard his words carefully enough, that the littlest ones could easily be questioned about things he said or did in class. Had she convinced herself that Leif was to blame for Mr. Jensen's arrest when he really had nothing to do with it?

Leif slumped against the back of the bench and stared at the sky. When he spoke again it was almost as if he were talking to himself. "I never asked for this occupation. None of us did."

Then he turned to face her and smiled wryly. "Except perhaps Quisling, and look how things are working out for him!"

She chuckled at that despite herself, which eased the tension slightly. A light breeze rustled the giant pine at the back of the garden and bits of snow fluttered to the ground. Mari followed Leif's gaze to the tree, then to the mountainside rising behind it.

It was Christmas Eve. Mr. Jensen's words came back to her. A gesture of peace felt appropriate, but she could never agree to his offer of friendship.

"This occupation can't go on much longer, Leif. Perhaps when it's over everything will go back to normal, and we can see if it is possible to be friends again."

He swung around to face her and propped an elbow on the back of the bench. "The occupation ending soon? I wish more than anything for *that* fantasy to be true."

She didn't appreciate having her hopes dismissed so quickly, but he could be right. Her hopes could be nothing more than a fantasy. She managed a weak smile and raised eyebrow.

He continued. "You're so often right, but not in this case. I've learned many things that never make it onto the radio or news reports." He paused, catching her eye. "I knew about the round-up of dogs before it was announced, remember?"

His advance warnings had given them time to work out a plan that saved Thor's life.

"News comes only when the Germans *want* to release it. And that includes the NS radio, *Fritt Folk,* even BBC reports or Jossing papers." He stared directly into her eyes.

She felt a moment of panic, as if he had accused her of distributing underground papers or having a radio. She forced herself to calm down, remembering it was commonly known that such things existed. Certainly this wasn't aimed at her or her family.

On the other hand, was he gauging her reaction to catch her off guard, to make her confess to something?

She sat still, breathing slowly and exhaling clouds of frost.

Leif sat up straight. He spoke softly and shifted to the edge of the bench, poised to stand. "I'm sorry, Mari. It's too cold for this talk. I hoped you might be as lonely as I am, or at least enough to renew our friendship. I should have known you are too strong, and yes, too stubborn, to change your mind about me."

She couldn't help but smile at that comment.

"But we could be living like this for much longer than we ever dreamed; years, even. If that's true, can't we find a way to . . . to get along? To remember who we were before this began? If not as friends, at least not as enemies? I could warn you of danger or help you protect your family. Some things I do might annoy you, even anger you, but they're meant for good, whether you believe that or not."

Mari sat up and faced him, as confused as she was annoyed by what he was saying.

"I'm just asking for the benefit of the doubt sometimes. You were furious when I said that you needed to grow up and realize that the world isn't black and white, that there *are* many reasons for the things people do and the choices they make. Whether you want to believe it or not, it's the truth."

Mari nodded and whispered, "I realize there's some truth in that, but it doesn't mean I can trust you as I did years ago."

"I can see that," he said, "but could we consider this a first step toward a truce? I won't change what you believe and you won't change me. But can't we both admit there are reasons behind others' choices we may not understand?"

Mari recognized the truth in that, too. She saw it in her own family and in the doctor, in households she visited and people in the village.

Leif rose and reached for her hand. She hesitated, a long pause, then finally took his hand and stood.

She stepped back enough to meet his gaze and said, "It's good we had this talk. I make no promises. But I will stop making assumptions and laying blame without knowing the facts."

"Well, that's not what I hoped for. But it's a start, and a Jul gift to me. Tusen takk, Mari."

Papa appeared around the corner and asked politely, "Ready for some hot tea, Leif?"

"Nei, takk, I'll go home now. God Jul to you and your family, sir."

"God Jul to you, Leif." Papa wrapped Mari under his arm and led her inside.

Mari leaned into her father, grateful for his strength, for something that felt solid and certain. Mama gestured to the place set for her at the table, but Mari felt too exhausted to lift a teacup. Instead, she said goodnight and headed straight to bed, eager for a long night's rest.

But instead of sleep, she lay awake for hours, mulling over the conversations and challenges of a very confusing Christmas Eve.

Chapter Thirty-Nine

New Year, 1943

First of January, 1943.

Glade Nytt År, Bjorn!

I've resolved to write the truth this year, the whole truth. It's a choice I've made, and I'll live with the consequences if they come. Half-truths and "official" versions of the truth cause more harm than good. It's been a difficult lesson to learn, and one I'm still working on.

I'm also trying to remember that people make very hard choices all the time and I shouldn't be so quick to judge them. I just wish you were here, Bjorn, so I could ask your advice when I get confused.

When Mama and Bestemor are working at the main house, I'm comfortable in the cottage. It's the nights, when they work in town or go to meetings, that time drags on and on. I worry about Leif or the soldiers coming by. For the most part they leave us alone, but I can't escape the feeling that someone has been snooping inside the cottage when we're all away.

Goatman is the worst. He appears out of nowhere and for no reason. If someone is up to no good, it's him.

When I told the family things I had seen him doing, Mama said other soldiers were mad at him, too. They blamed him for stealing holiday gifts and poking into their packages and mail. Papa just said we should expect such things from every one of them, since the squad of Germans in the house specializes in spy detection.

I used to enjoy time on my own, but visiting at Mrs. Nilsson's feels much safer than staying alone in the evenings, and it reminds me of old times. There's always something to laugh about. Last evening, New Year's Eve, I found them eager to offer a toast. Astrid's mother waggled her left hand in the air. The wedding rings she always wore, even after her husband died, were gone. A new ring was on her finger!

Mr. Jensen explained that they were toasting their "engagement." It's just a ploy to stop the new soldiers in town from pestering her to spend time with them. Mrs. Nilsson loaned them a ring she had saved for emergency bartering. Our happy toast for their future, even a pretend one, lifted my spirits.

My hopes for freedom in 1943 are confused, Bjorn. Our Julaften conversations about the tide turning against Hitler raised my hopes. I believed it was possible that next year at this time you'd be home, and I wouldn't need to write to you to share news. By then I wouldn't have to worry about who can be trusted and who can't, because the dangers would be over.

Then Leif warned me that based on what he hears from soldiers, he believes the Germans could be here longer than that. Much longer.

Maybe it's just more of their boasting, but he seemed so certain that things will get worse instead of better. It's a terrifying prospect. Am I just in denial?

When the invasion first began I made the mistake of believing we'd have a speedy end. But those hopes proved foolish. It gets harder and harder to let myself hope and believe. But without hope, what do we have?

Oh, how I wish I could talk to you and hear what you're thinking.

We've faced so many challenges and so much sadness in the past three years. I know my early hopes were foolish, but I've grown up since then.

What would you say if you were here, Bjorn?

Do *you* dare to hope?

Should *I* dare to hope?

Only time will tell.

For now, it's a new year—and I choose to hope.

END

Author's Note

This trilogy (*Odin's Promise, Bjorn's Gift,* and *Mari's Hope,* the third book to come) are historical novels. The characters and events are fictional. However, many of the events, dates, and anecdotes that are woven through the novels incorporate actual events. Historical references and a bibliography of my research materials are provided to help readers sort out fact from fiction. Additional specifics and links are on my website:

www.sandybrehl.com

Things you'll find there include:

- Timelines of the increasingly oppressive German occupation.
- Key events of World War II referenced in the novels.
- Details about formal and informal resistance operations.
- Laws imposed regarding Jews and a timeline of their arrest and movement to concentration camps, as well as information about eventual outcomes.
- Changes in school patterns and cultural restrictions.
- Events surrounding the collection of dogs for service in the military.
- A timeline of both historic and fictional events in

Odin's Promise and *Bjorn's Gift*. This timeline will be extended after the release of *Mari's Hope* in Spring 2017.

Additional content online describes sources for some of the anecdotes shared with me that are woven throughout the novels. You'll also find several scenes/chapters retrieved from "the cutting room floor," out-takes of a sort.

I hope you'll take a look, and I welcome your discussions and questions, which you can send to me via my Contact page on the website, or directly: sandy@sandybrehl.com.

You might note my decision, begun in Book 1, to use the boy's name *Bjorn* without the *ø* (an *o* with a slash through it) found in the Norwegian name *Bjørn*. This was to make the name more accessible to English-language young readers (where the form *Bjorn* is found in Norwegian-American families). However, I likewise chose to keep the umlauts in German words like *Fräulein*, to make the words seem more foreign to readers, as it was to the Norwegian characters in the story.

Glossary

To hear foreign words and names spoken by native speakers, you can find websites, such as www.acapela-group.com, where you can enter a word and hear it pronounced.

Norwegian Translation Guide

Akevitt (AH kah veet)—a strong alcohol, often made from potatoes, traditional in Norway. Similar to vodka.

Bestemor (BEST uh mor)—grandmother. Variations: *Mormor* (mother's mother) or *Farmor* (father's mother).

Bestefar (BEST uh far)—grandfather. Variations include *Morfar* (mother's father) and *Farfar* (father's father).

Bjorn (bee YORN)—in Norwegian, spelled Bjørn.

Bunad (BOO nahd)—traditional clothing from each region in Norway, worn on holidays and special occasions. Plural: *bunader* (but "bunad" was used for singular and plural in this story to avoid confusion).

Fjord (FYOORD)—an arm of the ocean that reaches far inland, combining sea water with fresh water melted from the mountains and glaciers.

Fritt Folk (FRITT FOLK)—Translated as "Free People," this was the official newspaper of the Fascist/Nazi party, (NS), published in Olso and controlled by Germany.

Glade Nytt År (GLAD-uh Nitt Or)—"Happy New Year."

God Jul (guhd YOOL)—Merry Christmas

Grini (GREEN-ee)—a prison camp near Oslo, used by the Germans to detain, question, and torture prisoners of war, especially those suspected of spying or reisstance activities.

Ja (YAH)—yes

Jossing (YOSS ing)—an expression used by Nazi sympathizers to accuse other Norwegians of being disloyal. It was adopted with pride by those who resisted the occupation. The secret (forbidden) papers with cartoons and other stories against the Germans were called the *Jossing* papers. (In Norwegian, it is spelled *Jøssing.*)

Jul (YOOL)—Christmas

Julaften (YOOL ahf tun)—Christmas Eve

Jule Nisse (YOOL-ah NEES uh)—a type of Norwegian Christmas elf or gnome, traditionally a small, seldom-seen fellow, now sometimes similar to the American Santa Claus.

Krone (KROH nuh)—a coin, the unit of currency in Norway's economy. During the war, metal was needed for weapons and ammunition, so paper "coin notes" were used.

Linge (LING ah)—a company of Norwegian soldiers, named for their commander, Martin Linge, who escaped to England after the German invasion; he trained men to return to Norway on secret missions during the occupation.

Mari (MAH reh)—a Norwegian version of the name Mary.

Nei (NYE)—no

Nei takk (NYE tock)—"No, thank you."

Nisse (NISS uh)—small Norwegian gnomes or elves. See "jule nisse" above. Plural: *nisser* (NISS er).

Norsk (NORSK)—Norwegian

NS—*Nasjonal Samling* (National Union) Party; the Nazi-based Norwegian party supporting Hitler's occupation.

NSUF—*Nasjonal Samling Ungdoms* (Youth) Force; for boys and girls age ten and up, created by Quisling to train Norwegian youth to support the Nazi party and the Germans. (Unghird was a subgroup, for boys ages 14–18.)

Rømmegrøt (RAHM uh grot)—rich sour-cream porridge, traditionally served on holidays and special occasions.

Sov Godt (SOHV gott)—"Sleep well."

Syttende Mai (SITT uhn duh MAI)—May 17. The date on which Lise and Erik married in 1941, this is Norway's National Constitution Day, celebrated much in the same way as the 4th of July is celebrated in the U.S.

Takk (TOCK)—thank you

Takk for maten (TOCK for MAH tuhn)—"Thanks for the food." It is the proper form of thanks used at the end of any meal or food served.

Tante (TAHN teh)—aunt

Tusen Takk (TOO zen tock)—"A thousand thanks" (a phrase used to show gratitude for something very special).

Unghird (OONG herd)—literally, "young followers." This

Norwegian youth group mirrored the German Brown Shirt Youth force. It prepared males 14–18 to join the elite military groups when they reached 18. There were also groups for younger children (10–14) and for girls, but this story focuses on the Unghird group.

German Translation Guide

Auf Wiedersehen (off VEE der zayn)—"Goodbye."

Aryan (AIR ee uhn)—in Nazi doctrine, anyone who has so-called "pure" white or Caucasian heritage. Nordic bloodlines were highly admired, while no African, Jewish, or other non-white ancestry was acceptable.

Danke (DAHN keh)—"Thank you."

Deutschlandlied (DOYSCH lahnd leed)—"Song of Germany," the German national anthem.

Dummkopf (DOOM kopf)—a stupid person

Führer (FYOOR er)—leader (refers to Adolph Hitler)

Frau (FROU)—Missus; title used for a married woman.

Fräulein (FROU line)—young miss, an unmarried girl.

Gestapo (gehs TAH poh)—the powerful Nazi secret police.

Guten Tag (GOO tuhn TAHG)—"Good day."

Heil, Hitler (HYL HIT lehr)—"Hail to Hitler." This is the official salute to Hitler, spoken with the right arm raised straight out and up in salute.

Hund (HOOND)—hound, any type of dog. Plural: *hunde.*

Nein (nyn)—no

Swastika (SWAHS tick ah)—the main Nazi symbol, a type of cross, originally a sacred symbol for "well-being."

Pronunciations of Locations

Bergen (BAYR gehn)—second largest city in Norway, on the western coast district. Bergen is Norway's major southwest harbor on the North Sea.

Garnes (GAR nuhz)—a village on the opposite side of Sørfjord from Ytre Arna.

Indra Arna (IN drah ARN uh)—a village across Sørfjord from Ytre Arna. *Arna* is the name of the district. *Indra* means "inner," on the side of the fjord closer to Bergen.

Oslo (OHZ low)—the capitol of Norway, on the southeast corner of Norway.

Sørfjord (suhr FYOORD)—"South Fjord," this is the innermost and longest arm of the Hardanger Fjord, which connects with the North Sea near the city of Bergen.

South Trøndelag (TRAHN duh lahg)—a district north of Bergen, reaching from the Atlantic ocean to Sweden.

Trondheim Fjord (TRAHND heym FYOORD)—a fjord that leads inland to Trondheim, the old capitol of Norway.

Ytre Arna (EE truh ARN uh)—the village on Sørfjord where this story takes place. *Arna* is the name of the district. *Ytre* means "outer," on the side of the fjord farther from Bergen.

For Further Reading

FOR YOUNG READERS (OR ANY AGE)

The Diary of a Young Girl, by Anne Frank and B.M. Mooyaart. Bantam Books, 1993 reissue.

The Book Thief, by Markus Zusak. Alfred A. Knopf. 2007 reissue.

The Boy In Striped Pajamas, by John Boyne. David Fickling Books, 2007 reissue.

The Boy Who Dared (novel based on the true story of a Hitler youth), by Susan Campbell Bartoletti. Scholastic Press, 2008.

The Devil's Arithmetic, by Jane Yolen. Puffin Books, 1990 reprint.

Irena's Jar of Secrets, by Marcia Vaughn. Lee & Low Books, 2011.

Star of Fear, Star of Hope, by Jo Hoestlandt. Walker Children, 1997 reissue.

Twenty and Ten, by Claire Huchet Bishop. Puffin Books, 1978 reissue.

RESEARCH BIBLIOGRAPHY

Billie Boyle: A World War II Mystery, by James R. Benn. Soho Press, 2006. (A novel, but an author's note in it led me to

Operation Jupiter, an Allied plan involving Norway.)

In the Shadow of the Gestapo: A True Story, by Astrid Karlsen. Scott. Nordik Adventures, 2008.

Folklore Fights the Nazis: Humor in Occupied Norway, 1940–1945, by Kathleen Stokker. University of Wisconsin Press, 1997.

My Sixty Years With Norwegian Elkhounds, by Olav P. Campbell. Show Quality Publications, 1988.

Norway 1940–1945: The Resistance Movement, by Olav Riste and Berit Nokleby. Johan Grundt Tanum Forlag, Olso, 1970.

Our Escape from Occupied Norway: Norwegian Resistance to Nazism, by Leif Teerdal. Traford Publishing, 2008.

Remedies and Rituals: Folk Medicine in Norway and the New Land, by Kathleen Stokker. Minnesota Historical Society Press, 2007.

The Shetland Bus: A WWII Epic of Escape, Survival, and Adventure, by David Horwarth. Globe Pequot Press (The Lyons Press). 1951.

War and Innocence: A Young Girl's Life in Occupied Norway, (1940-1945), by Hanna Aasvik Helmersen. Hara Publishing; Seattle, Washington, 2000.

We Are Going to Pick Potatoes: Norway and the Holocaust, the Untold Story, by Irene Levin Berman. Rowman & Littlefield Publishing Group, 2010.

# Acknowledgements

Bjorn's Gift (and the coming third book in the trilogy, *Mari's Hope)* would never have been written had not readers of *Odin's Promise* cared enough about Mari and her family to ask, "What happened next?" A writer hopes for no greater gift than to have readers to care and ask for more.

Though I had no plans to write a sequel, within months of Mari's and Odin's launch into the literary world, I began thinking about what *might* have happened during remaining years of the war. Readers of many ages asked questions about the first book, and connected me to survivors of the occupation of Norway who were gracious in sharing stories of those times. After an initial attempt to write a single sequel, I ended up dividing it into two separate books that better serve my characters and my readers.

My "writing sisters" helped shape the original story and were my first readers on my sequel attempt. I continue to be grateful for all the ways my writing improves by knowing Jenny Benjamin, Dawn Bersch, and Christa Von Zychlin. Jan Gustafson has also been a supportive reader whose suggestions strengthen my writing.

I'm especially grateful to the supportive members of Milwaukee's Sons of Norway lodge, Fosselyngen. I'm also deeply grateful to the Norwegian Elkhound Association of America for their warm embrace of Odin and his story. Barb Budny and Dr. Ann Becker pursued answers to any questions I had about *The Great Grays.* Karen Elvin gave me a copy of *Tallo,* the book she edited in English translation. It details the stories of Olav P. Campbell's long life in Norway as a breeder and champion of his beloved *Norsk Elghund* dogs, including his wartime experiences. The threats to Thor in *Bjorn's Gift* represent a modified version of actual events documented in Campbell's book.

I repeat my heartfelt thanks to a very dear friend for inviting me to share her family history and travels to Norway many years ago. Without her introduction to the people I met during and since those visits, these books would never have been written.

Tusen takk to my expert fjord-fishing consultant, Eugen, from Ytre Arna. His daughter, Mari, is the namesake of my central character.

My deep thanks to Irene Levin Berman, author of *We Are Going To Pick Potatoes* and *Norway Wasn't Too Small,* for her valuable suggestions to make the historic references about the treatment of Jews as accurate as possible.

Throughout my life, my family members have been my biggest cheerleaders, unfailingly supportive of my writing. Their encouragement and confidence mean the world to me. The same is true of friends near and far.

I can never thank readers of *Odin's Promise* enough. They opened their hearts to Odin and Mari, to their stories, and to her family's survival of the first year of German occupation of Norway. I hope they will enjoy learning what happened in the subsequent years of German occupation.